CELIA

ADDISON JAMES

ADDISON JAMES

To everyone told their love language is acts of service, and kills themselves to make others like them: take up space. You deserve it.

CONTENTS

Content Notes   VIII

1. Celia   1

2. Bethany   4

3. Celia   9

4. Bethany   15

5. Celia   22

6. Bethany   27

7. Bethany   33

8. Celia   38

9. Bethany   44

10. Bethany   49

11. Celia   52

12. Bethany   56

13. Celia   62

14. Bethany   68

15. Celia   73

16. Bethany   78

17. Bethany   83

18. Celia   88

19. Bethany   96

20. Celia   103

21. Bethany   110

22. Celia   114

23. Bethany   119

24. Bethany   123

25. Celia   128

26. Celia   134

27. Bethany   138

28. Celia   148

29. Bethany   155

30. Celia   167

31. Celia   177

32. Bethany   184

33. Bethany   188

34. Celia   194

35. Celia   198

36. Bethany   203

37. Celia   209

38. Bethany   214

39. Celia   220

Epilogue: Bethany   224

Also by Addison James   226

About the author   227

CONTENT NOTES

*Loss of family (off page) and grief

*Violence of the supernatural creatures fighting each other variety (up to and including death)

*Dislike-to-lovers

*Manipulative, coercive relationships (not between the main couple)

*Multiple on page explicit sex scenes

CHAPTER ONE

CELIA

The day of the funeral dawns gray and cold. It's the kind of gray that makes everyone want to hide in bed, that makes wolves want to curl up with loved ones in their den, that makes the world turn slower.

How appropriate, then, that we have to bury our parents today.

I've chosen a spot in the hills. I've chosen, because apparently that falls to me now. An accident of birth, a few minutes difference—a few minutes I'm not responsible for and will never remember—means that the entire pack looks to me for decisions.

No, not just the entire pack; all the werewolves are now looking toward me.

The four of us stand at the front of the pack, but I can feel the crush of people behind us. Everyone turned out today to say goodbye.

I force myself to stand a little straighter, because that's not entirely true. Everyone turned out to say goodbye to my beloved parents, but I know they also wish to see the untested new queen in action. It's a concerning thing, to suddenly have a regime change. When your rulers should reign for millennia longer, no one expects their untested daughter to take the crown while they should still be in their prime.

I'm barely seventy years old. I should have centuries left to learn from my parents. I should have years to visit the rulers of other species, learn their ways, and ingratiate myself with the wolves under my rule.

Someone twitches next to me. I don't turn my head, but I already know who it is. If I feel like a child standing here, then I can't imagine how Callum feels. Just twenty, he's too young to have lost his parents. The boy saw real violence for the first time in his life, watched his safe village be upended, and was forced to witness the death of his parents all in the same day. No one should have to live through that.

I ache to comfort him, but I can't move. Neither of us can appear weak in front of everyone. Callum is a man now. Too young, too soon, but true nonetheless. He's a man, and I'm a queen, and weeping graveside is unbecoming for both of us.

I look at the bodies lying in the earth. I don't know how I'm expected to go on without them, but everyone is waiting on me, nonetheless.

I take a deep breath, trying to ignore the smell of fire that I know is all in my head, then throw a handful of dirt onto the grave. Each of my siblings follows suit, and then the four of us step to one side as the pack follows after us.

Someone will have to shovel the rest of the dirt in later. Whose job is that? Should I know that? Was I supposed to pick someone?

I force myself to take a deep breath. Someone will sort it out. Surely not everything can fall on me. Not today of all days.

No, today they will excuse any minor lapse in judgment. But tomorrow, everything will change.

A hand lands on the small of my back, and I know without turning it's Bryce. Only he would dare to touch me right now. Only he would think to. I take half a step forward, putting myself between my siblings and the grave, out of his reach. It sends a clear enough message—to Bryce, to the pack, and to me.

***

We're the last people to leave the graveside, and when we return home, it's eerily haunted. It somehow feels bigger now, emptier. Food from days ago still sits on the table, and there's dirt all over the floor. None of us even attempt to clean it.

"What happens now?" Callum asks glumly, looking around the home that should still feel safe for him, even if I doubt it ever will again.

"Now? We have a coronation to plan." It's Bryce who says it, definite and final and settling like a heavy weight over our home.

CHAPTER TWO

BETHANY

The whole village is hushed with a sense of dread. Ames took twenty men with him and left yesterday, and everyone here waits with bated breath. The palpable, heavy knowledge of what he's doing seems to grab everyone and grind their life to a halt.

Everyone, that is, except my mother. As soon as she's convinced he's not immediately coming home, she shoos the three girls that I don't have the heart to get to know out of the house and drags me to her bed. I stand gingerly in the room, loathe to touch something that he might have also touched. I hate this room, hate what it represents, hate what he does to my mother here, but if she wants me to be here, then I'll be here.

She packs a tiny sack with food, a small knife, and some warm clothes, hands it to me, and tells me to leave.

"Surely this is an overreaction," I murmur, trying to make her see reason. It's not an overreaction, though. Ames is a lot of things, all of them bad, but he's not a liar. If he says he's going to kill the king and queen, then that's what he means to do.

Her lips press into a line so thin they practically disappear. "He will get us all killed, Bethany. Do you understand that? He'll doom this whole village for his ego. And I need you... I need you to be safe."

"We didn't do anything," I protest. I know she won't hear it. I know that she hardly cares and that she's probably not wrong. What we did or didn't do is unlikely to matter. But I still have to try.

She gives me an impatient look, brushing off my argument that we both know is worthless. "Someone needs to go," she says. Her eyes dart around like she's guiltily checking for someone lurking in the corners. "It's too late. No one can stop him, but you can at least plead our case. Tell them not everyone here wants what he wants. And even if they don't believe you... you'll be safe. Out of here, and out of the way of their wrath. Or Ames' wrath."

"You should come with me," I say again, because this will be bearable if we go together. But again, she shakes her head almost before I finish speaking.

"I'll keep him distracted. I'll be fine, darling. You know he won't hurt me."

I don't know that. He won't kill her, but there are lots of ways to hurt a person. But it's not Ames I'm worried about for once. If I can't stop the wrath of the new queen from landing on this village, then my mother will be just as much a target as anyone else here. Maybe more so, considering that, much to her dismay, Ames rarely lets her too far out of his sight.

"I will buy you time," she continues. "He might not notice you're gone if I... distract him. Go. Tell them everything you know, and plead our case. And whatever they say—don't come back. Make a home for yourself there. I know you can do it."

She knows I can do it because we've both done it for years. I can scrub pots and skin rabbits with the best of them, and I can do it all day without complaining, too.

"You'll find me," I tell her firmly. "As soon as things smooth over. You'll leave him and you'll find me."

She pushes at my arms, not making any promises. I've tried to convince her to leave him over the years, and she never promises. She always says it's too dangerous, but now she's pushing me to leave, protecting me from danger, and won't follow me. I want to fight her on this, to force her to promise me, but she doesn't give me a moment to speak. "You have to go now. Before the girls ask any questions or anyone else comes around. Go. Now."

I look at her for a long moment, memorizing her face even if I could recreate it blindfolded already. Then I nod and turn to go, giving her what she wants.

***

I've never been outside our village before, at least not in my memory. I wasn't born here, but I don't have any memory of living anywhere else. My earliest memories are of the same village I just left, so I just have to hope that I'm running in the right direction.

The sun rises in the east and sets in the west. I follow the setting sun through the woods, watching the shadows grow long around me and the animals that prefer the night emerge. They all stay away from me, sensing the predator inside me.

Humans, I've heard, stumble in the dark hours. I've never met a human that I remember, and I'm just glad that I didn't inherit that particular fault. My steps are sure as I move through the darkness, confident as I get further away from everything I've ever known.

The dawn breaks, and by the time I stop, the sun is high in the sky. It's not hot, not even with the sun's strongest effort, but it's at least not icy cold anymore.

I hear humans are susceptible to the cold nights. That, unfortunately, I seem to have inherited, and it takes me too long to stop shivering.

I keep walking until the sun sets, then suffer through another cold night. I grit my teeth, refusing to complain.

Who would I complain to? My mother stayed behind, prey to a murderer, so I could have this chance. She's counting on me. I shiver and I keep moving, because there's no other option.

By the time the sun rises and I'm starting to feel warm again, I hear voices.

I take a long, tentative sniff. Wolves. I rock on my heels, indecisive for a moment. I try to see if I recognize any of them—the last thing I need is to run into Ames. But this isn't a marching army; this is a stationary group, and a large one. I don't recognize any of the scents, and I relax slightly.

I force myself to put one foot forward. I can do this. I will do this. I will make this a safe place so that someday my mother can follow me here and have her own safe place. She deserves that.

I'll do whatever I need to in order to give her that future. I'll tell them anything and everything they want to know about Ames, and then I'll pretend that I never came from there, never heard of Stone Village, and I'll blend right in. I'll chop wood, cook, clean clothes and houses—whatever it takes to make them give my mother and me a safe home here.

I take another deep breath to draw in my courage, and that's when I smell it.

Mate. That's my mate, the captivating scent of fresh rain over the forest. The wolf in me perks up, pushing me toward that scent, toward the one person meant for me. I'm helpless to resist.

Like in a dream, I keep walking, unaware of where I'm putting my feet and probably making a terrible racket. I couldn't care less, keeping my nose in the air to keep taking deep inhales of that scent.

I stumble into a village that looks deserted. Fires are smoldering embers, and there's washing on that line. People have been here recently. They're just not here now, not even a single grandmother or infant. Where would an entire village of people go?

My whole world is consumed by that scent, so I keep chasing it, heedless of the strange village.

I finally hear voices once I reach the far edge of the village. My wolfish instincts press me forward, wanting to find my mate, but I have the presence of mind to wait, ducking behind a tree to see what is going on.

It looks like the entire village is here, gathered in a circle around an ancient-looking weeping willow tree right on the edge of the river. I frown, trying to determine what could possibly be going on, when I hear one voice rise over the whispered hush of the gathered crowd. "I, Celia, descendant of the oldest of the wolves..."

Her. It's her, and I can't resist my instincts any longer, taking a step closer.

CHAPTER THREE

CELIA

I can barely force the words out. I shouldn't have to say these words, not now. Not yet.

I practiced in private this morning, whispering them to myself when I went off to bathe. I, Celia, descendant of the oldest of the wolves, do solemnly swear to protect the wolves from now until my death. I accept your fealty and do swear to live in the service of this crown. I could say it naked and in a river, but I can't say it here, surrounded by everyone I know with a crown on my head.

My brothers all stand behind me in what should be a comforting show of support, acting as my eternal shadows. That's how everyone always thought of us; the future queen and her three shadows, the men who will swear fealty above and beyond what any subject would be required to and serve this crown in their own ways.

I don't know about my brothers, but I'd never thought about it too hard. It simply felt too far away. I assumed all four of us would be the shadows of our parents for centuries—millennia, maybe—to come, and this day would be far, far away.

But now I'm here, trying to force myself to say these words, trying not to wince under the weight of the crown on my head, trying not to be stifled by the bear-fur cape Bryce draped over my shoulders earlier. My brothers might be here, but they can't do this for me, and I feel even more naked trying to say these vows now than I did when I was literally unclothed this morning.

"I, Celia, descendant of the oldest of the wolves…" I manage to force the words out. My voice sounds weak and shaky to my ears. I hope no one else hears the tremor. My mother would be frowning if she were here; you never show weakness where people outside the family can see it. Not if you're us. Not if they rely on you to be steadfast and consistent.

But my mother isn't here, and that's the entire problem. Even so, I have to remember what she taught me. It's more important now than ever.

I swallow, trying to force the next words forward. I take a deep breath to soothe my frayed nerves, my first real breath since this all started, and that's when I smell it.

Mate.

When I was a child, I asked how you'd know the smell of your mate. After all, if we know our mates by scent, but everyone smells different, who's to say which one is your mate? My mother had looked affectionately at my father and just told me I'd know.

I know now. The scent of fresh berries, tart and sweet and just off the bush, fills my every sense.

I throw off the stupid cape and let the crown fall to the ground, moving through an increasingly loud crowd. I couldn't care less what they're muttering about. I spare enough attention to know that my brothers are still my shadows at my back, but other than that, my entire attention is dedicated to finding my mate.

I see her as soon as I break through the crowd. She's as thin as the swaying willow branches behind me, with coloring so light it looks like snow. Her eyes are a pale, glacial blue, and she smells like summertime.

I've never seen her before. I know every wolf who lives in this village, and I know many of the wolves who live in nearby villages as well. Perhaps she heard what today is meant to be and came for the coronation.

When I suddenly stop at her feet, I hear my brothers all skidding to a stop behind me and a muttered curse from Heath. I ignore them, just staring at the woman in front of me.

"Hello," she murmurs after a long moment of me staring.

Her voice, high and clear, breaks through all the nonsense in my mind. There's an audience at my back, and I don't just mean my brothers.

I'm not queen yet, even if only by technicality. I don't owe the masses a full view of this moment. Family is one thing, but including everyone is a step too far.

"This way," I murmur, barely resisting reaching for her to ensure she comes with me. My hand itches to hold hers, but I refrain while everyone is watching.

I set off for our family home, gratified when she falls into step beside me and my brothers behind me. At least we don't have to do this in public.

When we're in our home, Callum closes the door behind us all and I close my eyes and take a deep breath. I meant for this to be a private moment, for my brothers to wait outside. I suppose I should have known they'd never do that.

"What's your name?" I ask. Best to start with the basics.

"Bethany."

"Bethany," I try, and it tastes as sweet as she smells. "What village are you from, Bethany?"

She hesitates, which is never a good sign.

Heath takes a step closer. They've been standing by the door as if barring anyone from coming in or out, but now he makes his presence known. "Your queen asked you a question," he says, his voice low and menacing.

I hold up a hand. I'm not a queen yet, and this woman is my mate. If our parents had made one thing very clear to us, it's that you're never the ruler of your mate. Heath takes a step back, but I don't miss the sharpness in his eyes.

And it's not unwarranted, because Bethany bites her lip and looks down before admitting. "I'm fleeing from Stone Village."

The silence between the five of us is deafeningly loud. Stone Village. The separatists who murdered my parents. I can smell the smoke and blood again, and have to shake my head to make it dissipate.

Callum speaks first. "Fleeing?" he asks, and I'm immediately grateful to my youngest brother for finding the one word we need to make this situation tolerable.

She tilts her head. "I came to warn you."

"You're too late," Heath says sharply.

She hangs her head. "I know. I just... I knew I couldn't be here in time. I came. Whatever you need. I'll tell you anything you want to know about Stone Village. But I also want to speak on behalf of everyone there. We're not all like Ames. Most of us aren't."

Bethany has four wolves staring her down, and we haven't offered her any sense of hospitality yet. I look her over, and while I still notice the willowy, graceful beauty, I also notice the dirt and damp clothes. She's been sleeping outside, and we need to be good hosts.

"Have a seat," I say, nodding to the table once lovingly built by my father. The father that her pack leader killed, I think, before squashing the thought. "Bryce, can you find us some food?"

The food is disappointing, leftover stale crusts of bread. I put mine in front of Bethany, not hungry, and watch as she stares at it for a long moment before devouring the first piece.

"There's more," I tell her, even though I'm not quite sure there is more. Not here, at least. But it doesn't matter; someone in this village will have food, and I'll make sure my mate is fed.

Heath leans forward. "What can you tell us about the Stone Village?"

"I've lived in Stone Village since I was two," she murmurs. "I'm thirty-five now."

Half my age. She's closer to Callum's age than mine.

"Where were you before that?"

"I don't remember, but my mother says it was a human village. On account of..." She takes a shaky breath. "I'm half human."

Callum whistles. "I didn't know that was possible. I didn't think we could... you know... with them."

"Well, we can," Bethany says, curling an arm around herself and turning her head defensively, bracing for a blow. I should tell her one will never come here, but I don't.

"Stone Village took a half-human?" I ask skeptically. They don't seem like the type of place to tolerate differences like that.

"The story is they killed my father. They killed most of the humans in the village. Ames does that. It's easier to kill humans and steal what they have than to prepare for a winter yourself. And my mother, she wanted to keep me safe. So she made us a place in Stone Village. I'm not the only one, either. You'd be surprised about the people who end up there because they have nowhere else to go."

"But you left."

Bethany bites her lip. "I wanted to help. To help both groups. And I'm sorry for your loss, and—"

"Don't." I can't hear it right now, not from her.

She goes very still for a moment, then nods. "I came here to offer whatever help I can." She juts her chin out, trying to look brave even when I can see nothing but fear in her eyes. "But I want something, too. I want a safe place. I can work. I will work; I'm good at it. I can keep my head down, and I can make it worth your while to let me stay. For me and, eventually, my mother. I just need a home. A home that isn't there."

She says there with enough disgust that part of me is warmed ever so slightly. She hates them nearly as much as we do. As far as mating bonds go, that's certainly a start.

I put my hands on my thighs and stand, and each of them immediately follows me. I'm briefly worried that I'll have to deal with this for the rest of my life, but I have bigger problems at the moment. "You'll tell us everything you know about Stone Village."

She nods. "If you promise to protect my mother."

"If she didn't raise a blade to my people—and doesn't in the future—then I will." That is a lesson from my father—never make promises you can't keep. It's best to set realistic expectations.

Maybe her mother is only with Stone Village to protect Bethany. But maybe she believes what her leader does. If she does, there can be no mercy, not even for someone my mate loves.

"Fine," Bethany accepts what I give her. "What do you want to know?"

"Not yet," I tell her, extending a hand that she takes. "We have something we need to do first."

Chapter Four

Bethany

Celia drags me outside, and I feel the menace of her three brothers behind us. They're like her shadows, chasing her around. Once we're outside, she drags me back to the still-waiting crowd. No one has left, although the din of them talking is getting louder.

Celia ignores the crowd, walking forward like she knows they'll move for her. When she gets back under the tree, she drops my hand and picks up the cape and crown she dropped earlier. She hastily secures them once more, leaving the beaten metal crown crooked. "I, Celia, descendant of the oldest of the wolves, do solemnly swear to protect the wolves from now until my death. I accept your fealty and do swear to live in the service of this crown," she says in a rush. Even so, I feel a shudder passing over us all.

Is it my imagination, or does she stand taller, look stronger? Celia already looked like an immovable mountain, but now I can't imagine anyone stronger.

She grabs at my hand once more, her grip tight, and hoists my hand up for all to see. "On this day, I bring to you all my mate, Bethany."

The crowd, previously silent as the grave, suddenly can't stop talking, murmurs shooting through the crowd, eyes peering into my soul. Can they see what I am, where I'm from, that I have no idea what to do here, at Celia's side?

I cringe toward Celia, hoping for—I don't know what, exactly. Support, perhaps, or just someone to cover me from the scrutiny of the crowd. Instead, she steps away, shedding the cape and crown and handing them to one of her brothers before walking back toward the hall, the four of us following at her heels.

As soon as it's just the five of us, I murmur, "You could have warned me."

"Consider yourself warned," Celia says shortly. "That's what it means to be one of us. If you want our protection, that's the cost."

It feels like a slap to the face. If I want her protection? I'm aware that I haven't seen the strongest examples of mating bonds in my life, but I know enough to know that as her mate, her protection should be automatic. Her whole family's protection, really. That's what mates do. She protects me, and I protect her. And yes, I might be getting the better end of the deal right now—I know my protection isn't worth much at this moment—but that doesn't mean I'd ever put conditions on taking care of her.

I square my shoulders, ready to—I don't know what. A part of me wants to tell her to fuck off, but she's my mate, and she's not entirely wrong about me needing her protection.

Celia runs a hand through her short hair. "Listen," she says, casting a quick glance around at her brothers, who still haven't left us alone. "You and I will have time. We'll sort this out. But today, now—there are bigger issues. There's a war to fight, and we need to stabilize the pack."

So I'm an afterthought. That's not new or different for me, but it hurts nonetheless.

Celia turns partially away from me, looking at two of her brothers. "Tonight, we get all the information we can. Tomorrow, we go to war."

One of the brothers looks at me shrewdly, and I realize suddenly that information means me. And he's looking at me like he's not sure if he'll ask me for it or force it out of me.

I swallow. "I'll tell you whatever you want, but no one ever trusted me with anything," I warn them. "I didn't know about the attacks before you all did." That was a mistake, I realize instantly. Mentioning the attack here just makes the hostility grow thicker.

"Sit down," one of the men says, his voice low. He's not mean, but it's also clear that there's no arguing with him.

I sit down. The rest of them don't. I feel them looming over me, and I shift uncomfortably in the chair.

I don't want this to turn into any more of an interrogation than it already is. Maybe if I can show that I'm cooperative and that I'll give them what they want, then this will be easier. Maybe they'll stop feeling like they need to loom over and intimidate me.

"The village is about two days from here on foot," I say, "If I walked in a straight line."

"We know where the village is."

Right. "There's about a hundred wolves living there."

"Mid-sized pack," the one who told me to sit notes quietly, more to himself than to me.

"Less than a quarter are fighters. The rest of them don't know anything, didn't do anything."

"And yet, you're the only one we've seen leave."

"It's hard to leave your entire family," I snap, unable to help myself. "People don't want to leave their loved ones. And Stone Village... Ames is a terrible man, but I can't pretend that he doesn't protect the wolves there. And a lot of us need that protection."

"You left," Celia says quietly.

And I still feel wrong about leaving. Ames is a terrible person, and I hope he dies at Celia's hands. But I left my mother.

Like I said, it's hard to leave your family.

Celia stands a little straighter, and something in her eyes softens just slightly. "You'll give us what we need, Bethany. And then we'll be able to do this and spill as little blood as possible."

"Ames lives in a hall in the center of the village," I say immediately, because that is the best offer I'm going to get. "His most trusted people live close to him, like a last line of defense. But don't think that means everyone close to him is a traitor. Ames keeps innocent people around, too. He likes to use them," I warn, unable to fight the bitterness. "And they don't know anything. They didn't do anything."

"You think no one knew?" one of the brothers presses.

I shrug. "I doubt many people know. He took soldiers with him, and whispers of his plan leaked out, so some of them must have known enough to let secrets slip. But I already told you. I didn't know much." I dare to be a little bolder now that they all seem invested in what I have to say. "Would you sit down?"

To my surprise, they do, each pulling out chairs around the table. One is left empty, and I realize with a jolt that I'm sitting in one of their parents' seats. And one is still left open, a permanent marker of their recent loss.

I hold no love for Ames. He uses the people in his village ruthlessly, not caring one bit about the people he crushes to get what he wants. He'd killed my father because his pack didn't prepare for a hard winter. And now he's so power-hungry he's killing people and bringing vengeance down on the innocents in his pack. I would be thrilled if Celia killed him tomorrow and got her vengeance.

If only I could guarantee that's all that would happen.

"What does Ames want?" the youngest brother asks softly.

The others look away from me to give him sharp looks, but I think the question is valid. I've been asking myself the same thing. "He likes control," I say, looking down at my hands, thinking of all the examples I've seen. My mother, the girls, his meticulous need to manage every inch of his village—he is a man obsessed with control. "He needs people to look to him. And Stone Village was enough for him... but apparently it's not anymore."

Ames needs us to need him. In Stone Village, we don't eat without his say-so. He controls who works and what work they do. And everyone there knows they have no better options, so we let it happen.

The room is silent for a moment, and then Celia speaks. "Tell me more about security."

"It's called Stone Village for a reason. The wall is significant. Definitely the first thing you notice. And Ames likes to think it's impassable."

"But it's not," Celia surmises.

I look at her for a long moment, debating. "It runs along the river on one side, and there's a spot where a flood wore away the stones enough that a small section crumbled. And it just... never got fixed. We like it. It's easier to do the washing when you don't have to go out the guarded gate and all the way around to the river to do it. You have to cross the river to get there, but assuming you don't try to cross during a flood time, you can do it easily."

"You've done it," one of the brothers concludes.

"How do you think I got here?"

I think they're looking at me with a little more respect now, and I shift uncomfortably in my chair. I know the deal I made with them was that I'd give them this information, but being stared at like a tool makes me feel small.

Why does it feel so bad? I've been looked at like a tool my whole life. I've been a useful object, someone who could be ordered around without consequence or fear of retaliation. No one ever worried about using me, and it shouldn't be any different here.

But it is. I look to Celia, hoping for—I don't exactly know what. Some form of reassurance, I suppose. But it doesn't come. She watches me just as intently as her brothers do.

"What else?" Celia prompts.

I force my face not to show how much that hurts. "I don't—I don't know." I'm floundering, realizing abruptly I came all this way for nothing. I don't know anything. I never knew anything truly useful. And I'm way too late to stop anything that happened.

One of the brothers shrugs, then looks at his sister. "I can get a sense of the situation."

She hesitates a long second, but then nods once. "Do it. And Heath—be careful."

Heath gives her a quick nod back, then looks back at me. "Tell me more about Ames. More than he just likes control."

"He's a total bastard."

That prompts a snort out of the youngest brother. Celia looks at him, and he shrugs. "What? We're all thinking it."

"More than that, please," Heath says.

Well, at least he said please.

"I don't know. I don't talk to him even when I do see him. I serve food and clean clothes, all right?"

That isn't the whole truth, but it's not a lie, either. I sleep in his house, living with the parade of girls he brings through, keeping an eagle eye out for how he treats my mother, even knowing there's nothing I can do. But he doesn't tell me anything, and I avoid talking to him whenever possible. I didn't lie.

"So he's not a man who interacts with his people," Celia surmises.

I shrug. "He interacts with people when they have something he wants."

"Like what?" Heath presses.

"He hand-picks his soldiers. They get preferential treatment, always have. If they want something, and they're valuable enough to him, he ensures they get it."

"Anyone else?"

People he wants to bed, I almost say, but don't. It's the worst type of attention, and I don't want to tell them how I know.

Would they still agree to spare my mother if they knew she was in his bed? Or would they consider that a step too far, no matter how little choice she's had in the matter?

I'm not going to find out. If my mate can look at me like I'm merely an information resource, then I can look at her like a personal soldier to rescue my mother. I'll tell her only what she needs to know.

"Ames cares about soldiers," I say simply. "The rest of us merely exist to serve that end."

The four of them look at each other for a long moment. "All right," Celia says decisively. "That's a start, at least." She looks at each of her brothers, and then says, "Get lost."

"Celia—"

"Now."

What can they do but obey? She's the queen, after all.

CHAPTER FIVE

CELIA

"You didn't have to send them away," Bethany says quietly once the door closes behind my brothers.

If there's one thing I learned from watching my parents, it's that some things are just for the mated couple. The highest highs and the lowest lows are simply too personal to air in front of others.

"Yes, I did," I say simply, checking one last time that the door is closed before turning back to her. She looks tired and worn out, and I realize she likely hasn't slept since she left her home.

Her home. That fucking pack is her home. Or was her home, at any rate. And I doubt that something like Stone Village is forgettable overnight.

What kind of damage did that place do to her?

"What are you thinking about?" Bethany asks softly.

I flinch. It's not that I forgot she's here, obviously, but I'd been too busy thinking about what she represents to acknowledge her sitting in front of me. "Do you know what tonight is?" I ask abruptly instead of answering.

"Hard not to. Moonrise is in a few hours."

I can feel it coming, stronger than I could before. Is it the coronation or the new mate that does that to me, that makes me intimately aware of the rise of the full moon and what's coming tonight?

I don't know any mated couples who met with only a few hours to go before the full moon. That seems like a recipe for ruin. No one should commit eternity to someone mere hours after meeting them.

"Do you want to..." Bethany begins but then trails off, voice unsure.

"It's not something we can ignore," I say, trying not to snap. It's not her fault we're in this predicament, I remind myself. "The moon will rise, and then we won't have a say anymore."

She flinches slightly, then seems to collect herself. Good, I suppose. Being able to keep a calm, collected face is a mark in her favor. That's what's required to rule, and I'll need her at my side now that I've been crowned.

Dear gods above, who will accept her as the co-ruler of this pack? We can't keep her history a secret. She's a half-human from Stone Village. There's nothing about her a pack would want.

Then we'll just have to mitigate the damage. My parents were co-rulers, but nothing says my mate must rule by my side. She can be my mate and have nothing to do with the governance of this pack.

As the queen, I need to know where the boundaries are and be prepared to draw that line. I can fuck her. I can maybe even love her someday. But I need to learn how to keep her apart from things she has no business being involved in.

Bethany takes another deep breath to steady herself. "Fine, then," she says. "I hope we can spend some time together first?"

"For a little while," I confirm. "But I need to... there's a war to plan."

She flinches now. "Right." Her voice is quiet, weak.

"Are you opposed to war now?" I push. I know I shouldn't, but I can't help myself. She flinched. She dares to not fully support justice for my family.

"Forgive me for worrying about a war when I have people on both sides of it."

Her mother and... me? Does she mean me? I soften slightly, involuntarily leaning closer to her.

"Do you want a tour of the village?" I offer.

It takes her a second to look at me, but when she does, I see that her expression has softened, too. "I'd like that," she whispers, so I stand and offer her my hand.

***

I show her the basics of the village, although there's not much to show. The homes are scattered around the entire valley, along with little fields and animal pens. There's the river, but we'll see that better when I bring her into the forest.

There's still the scorched earth where the old goat shed used to be. I know the blood I smell there isn't real, the stench washed clean by the acrid flames and the dirt we all piled on top, but I can't stop myself from scenting it, anyway. I look over at the spot my parents died and stay away.

People give us a wide berth as we move around the village. It could be her, or me, or simply because I was not subtle about the new mating bond, and everyone knows moonrise is growing closer and closer by the minute.

It could be any of those things, but I feel their eyes on us. I feel the stares, the impatience in them. These people are waiting to see what we do next.

I don't want to give them a show, so I wait until we're walking along the river to do anything but point out the local sights. "What does it mean for you to be half-human?" I ask.

She stumbles half a step. "It means nothing," she says shortly. "I have a wolf, the same as you do."

That was never in doubt. Any wolf would be able to smell that on her. "And that doesn't answer my question."

"I'm not different. I don't need to be coddled or treated differently."

Impatience bubbles in my gut, needing the answers that there's no good reason for her not to give me. "And you still haven't answered my question."

"I don't know what makes me different. I'm the only way I've ever known how to be. I'm thirty-five but stopped aging a decade ago. I'm strong. I'm fast. I can keep up with wolves around me just fine."

It's not the whole truth; the defiance in her eyes and her voice makes that too obvious. But maybe I am pushing too much. Maybe she's been asked to give up enough things for today.

And it's not like I won't find out in due time. We're bound together forever and will be even more so by the end of the night.

And if her weaknesses hurt her? Then it's her own fault for not telling me. I can't look out for what I don't know.

"Fine, then," I acknowledge crisply, then start walking faster. If we're not going to talk, then that's fine. She can make that choice.

We both know how this night ends. Knowing each other before then is apparently not a priority of hers.

I've ensured that this little outing will end with the two of us in the woods, hopefully away from the village. Not that any wolf would be unaware of what the two of us will be doing tonight, of course, and no one would be stupid enough to interrupt. But there's a sort of nervous, twitchy feeling under my skin. It's both similar and different to how I felt this morning, taking my vows before all the assembled wolves.

We're getting closer and closer to moonrise. I can feel it, the pull of the full moon already heating my blood.

And she won't tell me anything about her. Does she even want to be here? Is she happy to be here with me, or am I just a convenient place to stay safe? And does it matter, either way? It's not like I'm in a position to sort out how I feel right now. My heart is filled with revenge and stabilizing the pack; there's no room for her or the idea of our future or anything else.

Fuck, why did it all have to happen at once?

Chapter Six

Bethany

I can feel the moon the instant it rises over the horizon line.

I can always feel it at the full moon, but it's never felt like this before. What used to just lessen my inhibitions slightly now makes my blood heat, my desire rise, and my body desperate.

I need her. I need Celia, my mate, and I need her now.

I need to touch her and taste her and know every single thing about her. I need to learn her body from the inside out, need to know how her skin feels on mine, and I need to consume her.

I've never been so hungry, so desperate and yearning.

It should scare me, the distant, most rational part of me in the back of my mind realizes. I've never done this before, never even touched another soul like this. No one in Stone Village wants the half-human, after all. And now I'm going to have sex with my mate underneath the full moon, out along the river bank, and I'm practically out of control of my own body. I should be terrified to do this now, with the mate I barely know.

Somehow, I'm not. For once in my life, I'm at ease, leaning into my mate, ready for whatever comes next.

Celia's hand lands in my hair, tugging to pull my head back so I have to look up at her. I'm tall, but she's even taller, and right now, with the light of the moon surrounding her, I feel like I'm looking up at a goddess.

"Mine," she rasps, and her fingers tighten in my hair, possessive and sure, leaving no room for doubt.

I whimper. Yes, hers. Fate has made it so; I'm hers, and she's mine, and we've been bound forevermore. We're going to bind our souls tonight.

Her grip on my hair, paired with her other hand pressing into my spine, makes me feel something I've never felt before. I feel connected, whole, somehow more than I've ever felt. This is what being a mate is. She's mine and I'm hers. This is home, and I'm starving for it.

Before I can say any of that, she grips my hair even tighter, then leans down and seals our mouths in a kiss. The kiss is bruising, biting—wolfish. I taste her finally, and the wolf in me is desperate for more, chasing her unique flavor, looking past the meal we ate earlier and looking for that taste that makes her *her*.

Her hand is still locked in my hair, guiding my head exactly where she wants me. I bristle at that, the wolf not liking being controlled when all we want is to explore our mate, but she doesn't let me go. Instead, she tugs downward, and I follow the pull, moving down to my knees and looking up at her.

Still surrounded by the moon, Celia couldn't more clearly be a queen if she tried. There's a nobility to her. I blink up at the new queen, a thousand times more confident and sure than she was this morning, and the wolf inside me melts for her.

This is our queen, our mate. Ours.

Thankfully, she doesn't leave me on my knees in the dirt alone for long, joining me and immediately grabbing at my clothes. I shed them desperately, eager for nothing between me and my mate. I need her, I need her, I need her.

Our clothes shed, she kisses me again, a deep, hungry connection that makes me want to consume her entirely. More. More.

I'm on my back in the dirt, and she's over me, straddling me, and she breaks the kiss. I whine, but then her lips are on my breast, nipping and licking her way to my nipple, sucking teasingly before once again moving down my body.

She moves lower and lower, and I've never done this before, but I know what she plans because the wolf inside me is demanding the same thing. I want to taste. To bury myself in that deep, intimate part of her, to know her that fully.

She licks through my folds, and I whine, torn between wanting more and wanting to change our positions so I can have my fill of her. Celia doesn't seem to notice, just pinning my hips in place and licking again, then again, taking what she wants.

She seems more confident than me, like perhaps she knows what she's doing and I should let her guide the two of us. But I ignore that, pushing her off me.

She sits up for a second, tilting her head and watching, looking incredibly wolfish as she takes in the situation. I'd explain to her, but I can't quite force out the words, so instead I move to try to taste her.

Celia moves faster than I can see, putting me on my back and hovering over me. Her hands and knees pin me there, and I growl, wanting my own turn.

She growls back, then snaps at my jaw, warning me to heed her. I whine, unsure what to do. While I'm struggling, Celia moves until she's level with my core once more, but she shifts so her sex is by my mouth, and I can taste her, too.

The wolf in me wants to howl. Yes, this—this is right. This is what we need.

I lean my neck up so I can taste her, her scent drawing me closer and closer like a lure I have no hope of escaping. I don't even try, desperate to know my mate in this way.

And the moment her sweet wetness touches my tongue, I lose all control, all sense of the rational side of my mind. I give into my instincts and taste.

***

I wake up to a chill of morning dew clinging to my skin and the lightest brush of sun peeking through the trees.

Dirt and sticks are on my hair and skin, and last night comes back to me in fragmented flashes. My mouth on Celia, her sweet taste consuming me. Her tumbling me over that edge and then doing it again and again. I wonder if she was trying to prove something or if she's simply that skilled. Either way, I did my best to give her the same kind of pleasure.

If I wasn't perfect last night, I'll learn. We have time, after all. Mates are forever.

I touch the side of my neck hesitantly, wondering if there's a moment that hasn't returned to me yet. A mating should be sealed with a bite, with a mark binding us together. But no. There's no bite.

We haven't even known each other a full day, I remind myself sternly. It shouldn't be strange that we take this at our own pace. We have so much time.

I open my eyes and look around because, in addition to not having a bite, I don't have my mate, either. I can still scent her, heavy and strong, but that could be the remnants of what we did last night.

But no. She's sitting up, watching me, fully dressed. She has her knees pulled up to her chest, her hands around them, holding them to her, and a pensive expression.

"Time to go," she says, and it feels like a rock in my gut as I move to follow her.

***

I expected—I don't know what I expected. Privacy, I suppose. A little time to ourselves, time to parse through what just happened between us with our more rational minds in control. At the very least, I expected breakfast and sleep, maybe even a bath.

There is breakfast, even if it's just the end of a loaf of bread sitting on the table that none of us touch, because Celia doesn't give any of us a moment's respite before she begins planning.

"Heath, you leave today. Find out what you can about Stone Village. I expect a plan as soon as you can get what you need."

I open my mouth, then close it again. I shouldn't contradict her, not when she's the queen, not when she so clearly does not want my input—

But no. She's going to get her brother killed, and in this one particular instance, I know more than she does. "Stone Village will recognize an outsider in an instant. Particularly now."

Heath snorts. "Don't worry. No one ever recognizes me."

It sounds like bragging, but none of the others contradict him. Celia spares me half a glance, simply says, "He can do it," and then doesn't look at me again.

I curl up into myself, tilting my head down to study the whorl of the wood grain on the table. I can tell that I'm not needed here easily enough.

"Bryce," she continues, "We need to stabilize the packs in the meantime. Show them we're... I don't know. Functioning, I suppose. Alive."

He nods. "Show them that you're in control, and that they're safe."

Celia snaps her fingers once. "Yes. That."

"I already have a plan."

"I assumed you might."

"And what about me?" the third brother demands.

"You stay here." Celia's voice is like a mountain: solid and immovable.

Apparently, he still thinks there is room to argue. "Celia—"

"Callum. You are a child. You will stay here."

A fist hits the table, and a chair pushes back. I look up enough to see Callum, the supposed child, storming away from the table.

He doesn't go very far, just walks to the other side of the hall and seems to take a second to collect himself. "This is my pack too, Celia."

Celia ignores him and turns her attention back to me. "Bethany?"

"Yes?" I ask, holding my breath. I don't know anything about assuring the packs that their queen is a solid, capable leader, but I'll learn. I don't know where to find the other packs, but I can follow. I'll figure it out.

"Keep him here."

My stomach drops out with just three words. Keep him here. Because I'm not going with her. I'm not helping her politically, and I'm not staying at my mate's side. I'm being left behind.

CHAPTER SEVEN

BETHANY

She's gone in less than an hour, leaving me alone in a big, cold home I don't know with a sullen child I'm apparently supposed to watch over. She didn't even show me where I should sleep before she left.

Bryce is right on her heels as they leave, and Heath has already slipped away, unnoticed by all. I hope he is as capable as he says; I wouldn't want to see what Ames does to a Crae sibling who wanders into his village.

I look at the bread on the table and sigh. "You hungry?" I ask Callum. I don't know where to acquire food around here, but if he can get me food, then I can cook it.

He just looks angrier. "I don't need you to check in on me."

I look him over. Celia treats him like a child, and he does look a little younger than his siblings. While they've all settled into immortality, there's still some youth left in Callum, an awkward gangliness that tells me he still has growing to do. But he doesn't look like a child.

A grown man would feel resentful about his sister forcing a total stranger to be his minder, I suppose. But a grown man could be politer about it.

"Fine, then," I murmur. "Pretend I want to eat and I don't know any of the rules or expectations of this place. How would I go about getting a meal?"

He pushes open the door. "I'll send someone," he says shortly and then leaves without another word.

I'm already failing at the one task my mate asked me to do. I have no idea where he's going; for all I know, he could be stupid enough to try chasing after his siblings.

But I also don't know what Celia expects me to do or what about me made her think that I had the power to stop her headstrong little brother, an actual prince, from doing whatever he wants.

I tip my head back, studying the beams of the ceiling without seeing them. Less than a day. That's how long it's been, and Celia and I didn't have a single true conversation. Not about this. Not about this place, this life, our future.

I can still feel last night on my skin, in my blood, the wildness the full moon draws from us like a lingering touch. I can't forget it, but it's not enough.

I can't feed myself. I don't know where to sleep or where the best place to bathe is. I don't know my chores here or who can be trusted or what duties are expected of me other than keeping Callum here, and I'm bound to fail at that too.

There's a knock on the door, even though Callum didn't close it behind him. I turn to find a portly, kindly-looking wolf in the doorway, holding a pot of something under one arm.

"Lady Bethany."

"Just Bethany," I correct, hurrying to stand to invite her in and help her with her burden. "Did Callum send you?"

"He did, Bethany." She sets the pot on the table after shooing my attempt to help away. She stands upright, surveying the space with a keen eye, and I wonder how often the people of this village see inside their leader's home. Have I inadvertently breached some etiquette already?

I'm torn between feeling bad and reminding myself that this wouldn't happen if Celia had just spent a day or two actually speaking with me. "Do you know where he went?"

"Who? Callum?" She shrugs. "To train, no doubt. Never seen a boy quite so dedicated before. He'll practice by himself for hours most days. Or, he would. Before." Her eyes grow dark, and she turns away.

That's what I'm afraid of. Not training—although if I'm right and he hasn't reached his immortality yet, then even training could potentially be dangerous to his health—but the idea that he might be so enamored with war that he marches off to follow his sister.

She's gone right back to looking around the space, lips pursed as she does.

I try to see it as she does, try to find the fault she's seeing. Yes, this is a big hall to be so empty, and yes, there's not a single sign of life. It's hard to believe that the entire royal family of six lived here, seemingly happily and together, before my former pack leader did what he did. I can see the emptiness she no doubt notes, but this is also a place of luxury I couldn't imagine for myself just a few days ago, so I'm not going to be the one who complains.

Of course, Celia didn't show me any of this place except for the table, so for all I know, I could be sleeping right here tonight.

"My name is Agnes," she says abruptly. "And I'm going to guess between... well, everything... that no one has quite shown you around yet."

It's on the tip of my tongue to protest, to say Celia gave me a tour yesterday. And she did, but very little from that tour will help me today.

"You'd be correct," I murmur.

"Then allow me. After you eat something, of course," she says.

I look at the table and wonder if there's a protocol for inviting people to this table. Then I decide that the family is gone, and they've left just me, and protocol can go hang itself for a few minutes. "Join me?"

***

Agnes is nearly six centuries old, smiles constantly, and is eager to tell me stories about my mate until she realizes that it's not quite drawing the reaction she wants from me. Yes, it is adorable and sweet to hear about a little girl covered in mud absolutely ruining her father's clothes, but I can't quite connect the image with the hard, cold woman who left me here a few hours ago.

Agnes clearly sees me floundering and wants me to have a way to connect with this family that obviously doesn't want me. That's kind of her, but I've already decided that it's not what I need. I need a way to make this village like me.

The Craes don't have to like me or want me. My original plan doesn't have to change. If I can make this village like me, then I can carve out a place for my mother and me here, whether or not Celia accepts me.

I push my empty bowl away, then remember my manners and collect Agnes' too, setting them aside. I know where the river is, so I can fetch water and wash up.

I look around the hall once more, trying to see it as Agnes sees it. There's dust and dirt everywhere, the toll of the recent tragedy clear across the place.

If Celia had her way, I'd go and find Callum. But he's a grown enough man, and I know that I'm not going to be the one to convince him of anything. If he needs me, he knows how to find me.

In the meantime, I have chores to begin.

CHAPTER EIGHT

CELIA

B ryce gives me yet another look that I can only assume he believes is
subtle.

It's only subtle if not saying anything out loud counts as subtle. As for
the rest—the furrow between his brows, the way he keeps looking at me like
he expects me to run away at any second—well, no one could ever mistake
my brother as discreet.

At least he doesn't get in the way of what needs to be done. And he
did me the courtesy of distracting me while I moved away from the village,
pulling out his meticulously kept map of all the wolf villages. There are ten
of them, including both our own and Stone Village, so I have to visit eight to
ensure the transition from my parents' reign to my own.

Bryce rattles off information about the different packs as we travel,
prepared for this. He's always been good with information. I wonder how
long he's been preparing for this. While all of us did various diplomatic duties
while our parents were alive, Bryce was never asked to take on this type of
role. Did he always assume this would eventually be his future?

I don't ask. Talking specifically about the future, the death of our parents, and our new roles just among ourselves, feels too raw.

Unfortunately, we can't escape it within the packs. Crescent Moon Village is the first of our stops, and we spend the day speaking with local leaders. Their concerns about such a new young queen are barely veiled, and I grit my teeth as I listen.

"It's been a long last few winters," Terra, the pack leader, tells me.

"It has been colder than normal," I admit, only for her to look at me like I'm a toddler.

"It's been a hungry last few winters," she emphasizes slowly. "Our stores aren't quite going far enough."

I shrug. "So, what adjustments have you made to prepare for this winter?"

The room goes deadly still, and I feel Bryce next to me practically holding his breath. I know I'll hear all about what he wants to say later, but I also know he won't say it in front of these people. "What can we change?" Terra asks after a moment, voice bitter. "We need to eat in the summer, too. And we're not that big a village."

"You're not the smallest."

She ignores that comment. "The fact is, we can only do so much for ourselves. And North Star Village across the mountain trades with us sometimes, but they're even smaller than we are. Human villages seem to be our best options."

I think unwillingly about Bethany and her story, of Ames slaughtering her father's entire village. "Humans don't have anything we need," I say sharply.

Terra's second in command, a stick-thin boy named Allister, shrugs. "Sometimes they do," he says, looking me square in the eyes and refusing to blink.

"We keep to ourselves," I pronounce. "And this winter won't be any worse than the ones in the past. No need to catastrophize. We'll just start planning better."

I'm already getting used to my orders being obeyed when I say them with enough confidence, and no one here outright contradicts me. But the tension in the room doesn't ease.

***

"If you have something to say, then say it," I tell Bryce once I'm reasonably assured we're alone. We've been given a bedroom in Terra's home, so I keep my voice down. I'd be a fool not to think that no one is trying to listen, and I'd be a fool to make my weaknesses public, but I know this conversation is unavoidable.

Bryce rolls his eyes at me, and it strikes something deep inside me that, other than Callum's little protest, this might be the first sign of disrespect anyone has shown me since my parents died. It's good to know that my brother is still in there.

"How are you holding up?" he asks, which isn't what I expect to hear from him at all.

"What do you mean?"

"Your mate. Listen, I'm not an expert, but I watched our parents our whole lives. They could barely stand to be parted for a day or two, and they weren't new mates. So, how are you, Celia?"

"Fine." The answer is short, clipped, and a total lie. I've never lied to Bryce before, not about anything real.

He purses his lips. "Should we consider bringing her—"

"No." I hope that, for just a moment, we can go back to him treating me as his queen and my word as law. I don't want to discuss this.

And when it comes to Bethany, my word is law. No one else in the pack has any claim to her, and certainly not more claim than I do.

Unfortunately, Bryce has chosen now to break the spell my crown seemingly cast over everyone I know. "You're setting yourself up to hurt, Celia."

"I'm setting myself up to do my duty," I correct.

"And she can't be a part of that?"

Damn him. I take a deep breath and listen for a moment, trying to place everyone else in this home. I don't think anyone is standing right outside our door, but I lower my voice, just in case. No sense in spreading my weaknesses any more than I already have. "She's from Stone Village and she's half-human," I whisper furiously. "What about that makes you think this is a good place for her?"

He shrugs, as though I didn't just say two of the most damning things possible. "The fact that she's your mate?"

He says it like it's incontrovertible proof of something, and I haven't seriously wanted to smack one of my brothers in years, but I'm considering it now.

"What does her being half-human mean?" he asks.

"She wouldn't tell me."

He considers for a second, then shrugs. "I suppose I can't blame her. We just met her, and the first thing we did was interrogate her."

He makes it sound like we tortured her, but she came to us with the plan to give us all the information about Stone Village she knew. He doesn't need to make it sound so sordid.

I wonder if Heath has made it to the village and, if he has, if he's made it inside yet.

Were I not a new queen, he could easily slip in and assassinate Ames for me. I've heard Ames is a paranoid bastard, careful and meticulous with his security. Perhaps he is, but I know Heath is cleverer than him.

But I am a new queen, and I can't have anyone seeing weakness. An assassination is underhanded. If the packs are going to believe my power, then I need proper revenge for my family, and that means a brutal, public, and fair fight.

"It's just going to hurt you both," Bryce says, cutting across my thoughts and not letting me think about the bigger problems I need to handle in peace for even a moment.

I shrug, refusing to indulge this. "Things hurt," I say simply. "That is a reality of life. We deal with it and do what needs to be done."

He gives me a long, judgmental look, but he's either run out of retorts or my crown prevents him from saying what he wants to say. He turns away from me, leaving me to get a few hours of sleep before I return to my duty.

***

I sleep like shit, and I tell myself that it's just because I'm in an unfamiliar place. An unfamiliar place, surrounded by people I only trust in the most tentative sense of the word, after a very stressful few days. Not sleeping would make sense in that situation.

I don't remember much of the night of the full moon in the traditional sense. My wolfish instincts were far too close to the surface, leaving the night a series of impressions and emotions, flashes of moments woven together to give me a mostly clear image of what happened. What I do remember is feeling more rested than I ever have in my life when I woke up, with Bethany's nearly white hair spread over my chest while she dozed there. We'd slept in the dirt and sticks, completely naked and exposed to the elements. We'd been sweaty and sore and wrung out. We'd been strangers, essentially, and I'd had misgivings about her a mile wide. None of that changed it being the best night's sleep of my entire life.

And now, I toss and turn until dawn comes, no doubt keeping Bryce up half the night even if he's too reserved to complain about it.

When we both wake to begin the day, he gives me a long, judgmental look that I do my best to shrug off. I don't need to hear anymore of his thoughts on how this trip will go.

CHAPTER NINE

BETHANY

I feel like I'm stumbling around in the dark, but I eventually find a bucket and a rag. I walk over to the river to fill the bucket, then lug it back and set to scrubbing. It takes the rest of the day, and I'd hoped it would keep me too busy to think about anything else. Unfortunately, this type of cleaning is physically taxing but mentally freeing, and I have plenty of room for thought.

I refuse to let myself think about Celia. Celia is a nuisance who makes my heart ache. Celia made her thoughts very clear, and if our mating bond isn't a priority for her right now, then that's fine. I can take the hint and set it aside, too. After all, I didn't come here to find a mate.

I squeeze the rag extra hard and remind myself that I'm not thinking about Celia.

Instead, I shift my focus to think about this pack. Cleaning this hall is all well and good, but Agnes' reaction makes it very clear that this is typically a private space for the family, and almost all of them are gone right now. Callum is still here, but I doubt very much that there's anything I could do to win his approval.

So this is a start, and something to keep me busy today, but I need a better plan for tomorrow. It won't be difficult; I know what I'm good at, and I'm skilled at exactly the type of labor that a pack appreciates having done. I just need to learn the social ins and outs here; who to speak to, who to flatter, and who will be able to give me the resources I need.

I can skin a thousand rabbits, but I have no idea how to hunt them myself. I'd never been allowed into the forest to learn.

Callum could likely hunt the rabbits for me, and maybe that would be a fair trade to get him to tolerate my presence. Unless the minutiae of ensuring there is food on the table is beneath a prince like him; it had certainly been beneath Ames.

The stew Agnes brought was good, so no doubt she knows who I should ask.

I can chop wood, clean and mend clothes, and do a thousand other tasks as well. I just need to keep my ears open, see who needs them done, and find my way to fit in.

***

Callum re-enters the home with muddy boots just as I'm finishing beating out the rugs outside.

He stops dead in his tracks, which I suppose controls the mess enough for it to be manageable, although I'll need to trek all the way back to the river for more water. "You... cleaned."

"Yes."

Something interesting happens with his face, a battle of emotions. Finally, he settles on a sneer. "Our home not good enough for you?"

I don't respond. His insults have nothing on Ames, I remind myself. I have a purpose here.

He doesn't seem to like my silence, his expression growing uncertain as he shifts his weight from foot to foot. "I'm going to bed," he announces, like I have any say or any care.

I was told to look after him. Maybe he thinks I do care about information like that.

I don't know how old Callum is exactly, just younger than me, but he's not a child, that much is clear. I couldn't care less when a grown man chooses to sleep. So I just nod and finish with the rug while he walks away.

Then I get the bucket to return to the river for more water.

***

After I finish scrubbing the floor Callum walked on, I'm struck with the issue of sleeping once more.

The muddy footprints leave off on one door, so I know this is Callum's room. But I'm not going to go through the others to find Celia's, especially since she never invited me there in the first place.

In Stone Village, that type of impudence would undoubtedly get you beaten. And while I doubt that the average member of this pack would beat me after Celia so publicly announced that I'm her mate, there's no saying what the royal family themselves will do.

But I need to sleep. When was the last time I slept, really slept?

Last night comes to mind, flashes of touch and heat and passion, and then the soothing, warm, surrounded feeling that led to such deep rest.

Last night might have felt restful, but it was undoubtedly short and on the forest floor. While I'm not looking for luxury, I am hoping for a little more than that.

But not at the cost of undoing the work I've only started to do here. Grudgingly, I trudge back out to the main room of the hall and make do with what I have.

***

I wake up with Callum leaning over me, a frown on his face. "You slept out here?"

Obviously. I stir from in front of the fire, long since gone out, trying to subtly stretch all my limbs to shake out the ache of sleeping like this. I doubt a proper wolf would feel it, but I certainly am noticing the discomfort.

"Would you like breakfast?" I ask him instead of answering.

He opens his mouth, then closes it again. "Do we have any food?"

Unlikely, unless he went out while I was sleeping. But I need him to show me how to go about acquiring what I need. From there, I can handle ensuring we're both fed every day.

I push myself so I'm sitting upright, then turn to the fireplace. We're running low on wood, too. That's another task I can handle later, but for now, I can at least get a fire started.

Callum, to my surprise, sits himself right on the floor next to me. "I think we got off on the wrong foot," he murmurs.

I hum, not willing to confirm anything in particular. I want to stand up and get off this cold floor—even through the freshly beaten rug, the cold is undeniable—but now that Callum is sitting next to me, it would be the height of rudeness to get up and walk away.

He's silent for a long moment, but he's not ignoring me, and I get the sense that he's parsing through what he wants to say. I wait him out.

"I don't need a minder," he says at last. "Or a maid... or a mother." His voice breaks slightly on the last word, even as he tries to pretend it doesn't.

"I'm an ineffective minder at best, and I'm not your mother," I tell him quietly. As for the maid—well, I spent all day yesterday cleaning his home, so I suppose I can't quite shed that allegation yet. But I didn't see him cleaning, and someone had to do it. "Why don't you tell me what you want, Callum?"

He's quiet again. "I'm sorry my sister left you here," he says, which is not an answer, but it at least feels honest.

I shrug. "She has things to take care of." Because whatever else, I'm not going to air my feelings about Celia to her brother. That's our business. Celia didn't take any time to go over the rules with me, but I can see how this will work. She's queen, and she announced me as her mate to the pack. She probably thought that was protection for me. Therefore, I need to protect her and her business as well. That's how a good mating bond works; we look out for each other.

"What do you want for breakfast?"

"I'll eat anything. And if you show me how things work around here, then I can take care of it in the future."

He looks me over. "Alight, then. Follow me."

CHAPTER TEN

BETHANY

Callum knows everyone in the pack who will be willing to barter with me. Soon, I have everything I need to make bread, and Callum got it all for me with the promise of some chopped firewood. I'm surprised that he has to negotiate like everyone else, but maybe the youngest prince doesn't get all the privileges of royalty.

I set to making bread. It doesn't help with the lack of food right this moment, but if Callum isn't going to complain, then I'm not either. Watching Callum barter this morning has given me a good grasp on what kind of things are needed around here, and by tomorrow, I'll have what we need.

"I need to go," Callum announces, emerging from his room with his boots on and a sword strapped to his hip. I blink at it, hesitating, hoping this isn't where he tells me he's going after his siblings.

What can I do to stop him if that's what he says, though? The answer is nothing.

I don't know if he hears my worry or if he planned to say it regardless, but he says, "I'll be back when the sun goes down. Before I go... you must be tired." Exhausted, but I don't dare say that. "Come with me a second."

I set aside my half-formed dough and follow him. He leads me back toward the bedrooms, swinging open one of the doors. "This one is yours."

I peek inside. This one is Celia's is what he means, because although it is fastidiously neat, there are still signs of her everywhere. That's her scent that lingers in every inch of this room, inescapable and sure.

"Get some sleep," Callum orders in the way only a prince can. "I'll see you tonight."

***

Sleep is tempting, but I avoid it.

I like to think it's because there's too much to do. I need to ingratiate myself with people here, and I need to learn how to be a part of this pack.

I like to think that's the reason. It should be the reason. But there's also a persistent part of myself that's not sure how I feel about sleeping in Celia's bed.

I should want it. The scent of one's mate is supposed to be comforting, and I can't deny that I could use comfort.

But I don't want to steal it. I don't want to slip into her space without permission and take her scent. I want Celia to give me that comfort of her own free will.

It's a foolish thing to want. Celia made her feelings perfectly clear when she left. She'll claim me as her mate to her pack to keep me safe. She'll interrogate me because I'm useful. She'll sleep with me under the full moon because that's what mates do. But she doesn't actually want me.

So when Callum returns at dusk, the bread has been made, and I've acquired vegetables and a rabbit to prepare for dinner. There's a roaring fire and a heap of firewood beside it. I cut enough for us and to repay what Callum and I owed for the bread, and tomorrow I'll cut more for the rest of the food. I'd found the axe in plain sight in the hall, so I'm glad to know they trust me enough to leave me the weapon.

That wouldn't have happened in Stone Village. I'd chopped plenty of wood there, but since it required leaving the wall, it had always been a rigorously supervised activity. Not that the guards supervising us would help—they'd just watch us struggle, although perhaps I struggled more than most.

I'm not so much weaker than the average wolf, but I can't pretend that my muscles don't ache sooner, that I don't tire faster. So I've become very good at pretending because I can never, ever let anyone know that.

"Did you rest at all?" Callum asks, looking over what I've done, once again trekking mud inside.

"I like keeping busy," I deflect. "Dinner?"

He looks at me and frowns, but he doesn't argue.

***

I sleep in Celia's room that night. Her scent soothes me, and I drop into a deep, dreamless sleep for hours, basking in some sort of fantasy of our future, where we'd be in this bed together, where I'd be making dinner for the two of us, where she'd appreciate that, and we'd hold each other in this bed after.

And when I get cold and wake up because being cold shatters the fantasy—it's impossible to be cold with a wolf in your bed—the scent feels more like a tease than a comfort.

CHAPTER ELEVEN

CELIA

"Get your shit together," Bryce whispers furiously.

It's good to know how little time it took Bryce to get over me being crowned queen and be back to his normal self. I did worry for a moment that he'd never speak to me like this again, but I shouldn't have; he's back to being an ass whenever he feels justified, which is always.

"I'm trying." I shouldn't admit that—queens don't try, they just do—but if Bryce can tell me to get my shit together, then I can admit that I'm not perfectly above it all to him. If I can't tell him, then I'll never be able to say it to anyone.

"Try harder."

We are definitely past any reverence for the crown.

I can't entirely blame him, either. I know I haven't been my best self, and I was trained better than this. I've been preparing to be queen since I was a toddler, and just because we all assumed we'd have a lot longer doesn't mean that I have an excuse to fall apart now. I can do this. I should be able to do this.

I've been losing focus during conversations, missing details, and misre-membering who people are. I'd like to blame it on poor sleep, and perhaps that is a part of it. But the bigger part is the aching hole behind my ribs, like while I attempted to sleep last night, someone scooped out my innards with a spoon and then carefully sewed my ribcage back up around the empty hole.

Our parents always said you felt your mate like a rope knotting the two of you together, and if this is the pain from letting that rope stretch too far, then I have no idea how I'm supposed to live my life.

I'm going to have to go home earlier than intended, and that will create chaos in Bryce's plans. I know he's put a lot of thought into how best to introduce me as his queen, and I'll trample right over his efforts. The villages I'm ignoring might feel slighted, and I worry that might cause them to turn to Stone Village. Not to mention, if Heath returns with information for us, then we'll have to strike fast, and I might complicate things if I don't yet have all the wolves behind me.

I have to collect myself. Too many people are counting on me keeping it together, and I cannot let them down now.

"Fine," I mutter just to him before turning to the gathered crowd.

Half the village is assembled here, waiting for whatever I'm going to say. I know what Bryce wants, the reassurance he's hoping I'll give them. My job is to make them see that I am a continuation of our parents' reign in all the best ways. My job is to convince them we're a better alternative to Ames and the Stone Village pack.

"Right," I tell the assembled village. "Let's keep things simple. Nothing is going to change. I've been at my parents' side for more than half a century, and I can follow their rule. I know how to manage the packs. If your pack remains loyal, I will let your local leaders manage your day-to-day living." I take a deep breath. "But if your loyalty is in question—if you hurt other wolves—then I will do the job fate has bestowed upon me and enforce order."

There's so much silence in the room that you could hear a pin drop, and I can feel Bryce's pounding pulse like it's my own.

My parents never would have even contemplated ruling through fear. During my lifetime, they never seemed to struggle at all to get people to follow them. But while I am afraid—while someone came to my home and murdered my parents in a place that was supposed to be safe, while they tore my youngest brother's childhood away, upset the sanctity of our home, and forced me into something that I was simply not ready for—I don't know any other way to be.

***

Bryce pushes us to leave the village quickly.

And then, once we're on the road once more, he rides ahead of the four guards we have with us, and I know he intends for me to catch up to him. Riding ahead of the guards defeats the point of bringing them, but I like to think that they're simply overkill and that Bryce and I are perfectly capable of protecting ourselves.

Then again, our parents probably thought so too.

For now, I catch up to my brother, leaving plenty of space between us and the guards. This conversation is for our ears only; it will already be uncomfortable enough to admit my failings to my brother. "I know I didn't do what you wanted."

He barks a laugh, cold and a little bitter. "What I want apparently means nothing anymore, Celia."

More than a little bitter, then. "If you want something said a certain way, then you say it."

"I can't because by an accident of birth, you were born first, and I don't envy you what comes with that one bit," he says lowly. "But our parents always believed fate wanted there to be three of us—and someday four. We are supposed to support you, Celia."

I bite my tongue before I say things I regret. I don't feel very supported, but that's not Bryce or Heath's fault. Bryce is right; they can't take on this burden. And they'll never know what it's really like.

"If you have something to say, then say it," I snap. We're not doing this, not spending time discussing our birth or our expectations. Those roles have been set for decades now, and that's not the concern here. "If you don't like how I'm handling this—"

"I don't," Bryce interrupts, a refreshing bout of honesty. "But I think you already knew that, so me saying it surely doesn't say anything. Celia—you understand my point of view?"

"I understand you're going to tell me."

He stares at me for a long, long moment. The silence is aching and delicate, and I find myself holding my breath. "If you break something that has existed for thousands upon thousands of years, then it won't be because we didn't try to support you." And then he urges his horse a little faster, leaving me behind.

CHAPTER TWELVE

BETHANY

I wipe sweat off my brow after I finish hauling yet another armful of chopped wood. This should be the last one for today, at least.

No one's stopped me from walking straight out of the village and into the forest to fell trees as needed. No one seems to notice what I do at all, which is a novel experience. No one noticed me with interest at Stone Village, but I was always watched. But here, people will speak to me with mild interest, but no one watches what I do.

I pull my long hair off my neck, holding it up for a moment so the crisp air can cool me. When I feel mildly better, I take the wood I need to light the kitchen fire and haul it into the house.

Most of the wood I've cut is payment for the food scattered on the table before me. Agnes' neighbor Brenna even skinned the rabbits she caught me, a generous gesture that went above and beyond our bargain but will save me so much time.

It's already later in the day than I wanted it to be, but I'm not going to let that stop me from doing what I want to do today.

Callum has been gone since just after dawn, but I've stopped caring about that. Callum might be young, but he's grown, and he's not stupid. He's not going to run after his sister. I don't know what young princes do with their days, but I've decided it's not my business. He can do what he wants, and I'll do what I have to do.

Namely, building a place in this village for my mother and me, whether or not the Crae family decides to keep me.

Agnes and Brenna and a few others will have already spread word of what I promised them earlier, so I set to work making the largest meal I've ever cooked, and that's saying something. I cooked for just about everyone in Stone Village, but there was always a group of us working together. Today, I'm working entirely alone and feeling the strain of it.

How can the hall possibly get this hot this quickly? I've shed layers down to my underdress, hoping no one walks in until I finish this.

I get a stew put together and as much fresh bread as I can physically force myself to knead. I get the fire banked to a more acceptable level, re-dress myself appropriately, and throw open the doors of the hall.

Agnes sees and comes over, her own bowl in hand. "How'd your cooking go?"

"See for yourself." I beckon her inside, then ladle her a bowl of stew and cut her a piece of fresh bread.

"You know, any of us would be happy to help you."

I'm sure they would, and it's all because they have an idea in their minds of who I should be to their pack. Celia, after all, had held my hand and announced who I was to her moments after her own coronation. It would be hard not to draw conclusions after that, and I can't blame anyone for thinking how they do.

But I'm not going to take advantage of it or rest on honors I haven't earned. I'm not the queen of the wolves. I'm the one who chops wood and skins rabbits and does laundry, and none of that will ever change.

"Tell me if it's any good," I say instead of acknowledging what she said.

She sips from her bowl and smiles at me. "It's good, dear. I'll remind the others to come see you."

Brenna is next, taking a bowl as payment for her rabbits in addition to the firewood I brought her. She gives me a smile, too. "You share a bowl with me, and I'll always bring you a fresh catch," she promises.

Then she and Agnes send others. I feared no one would come, that no one would want to make time for someone like me, but there's a line out the door. No one stays, and I don't invite them to stay in a home I barely feel comfortable in, but most people eat a bit before they leave and give me a smile, at the very least.

I'm sweating again and just hoping no one else sees it. Who ever heard of a werewolf dripping sweat? Not me.

When I'm getting toward the end of the pot and worrying about soon needing to turn people away, I hear a grumpy bark outside the hall, and then the broad-shouldered form of Callum makes his way through the line. "What the fuck is this?"

"Dinner," I tell him. "I saved some for you."

"We feeding the whole village now?"

"And why not?" I challenge, stepping back from the pot and his imposing presence to look him over, trying to judge how angry he really is.

He huffs. "Are you under the impression that people here need charity?"

"I'm trying to get to know my neighbors," I say. "I saved you a bowl."

He looks at me for a long moment, and the crowd seems to pick up on the tension around us. I thought things were settled when he showed me Celia's bedroom, but evidently not. Sensing that, the crowd leaves the hall with all haste, leaving just Callum and I standing there.

I force myself to hold firm, or at least not immediately back down. I didn't do anything wrong. Feeding people is the opposite of something wrong. And considering the turmoil this village has been through, maybe someone else should have thought of this first.

I prepare a bowl for him. It's not the last of the food, but it's close. My stomach growls and I realize that I haven't eaten yet either, so I make another bowl for myself.

"Is this what you did in Stone Village?"

"Close enough. It was less... welcoming there," I explain.

"Less welcoming?"

"It was not about doing something nice for the people who live near me." I laugh, thinking about what an understatement that is. "Stone Village isn't like that, particularly if you're like me."

"Like you?"

"Not someone in Ames' favor. Ames really only kept me because of my mother. And because you need someone at the bottom of the pecking order. Someone who can cook the meals and wash the laundry and everything else."

Callum freezes with his spoon halfway to his mouth. "Is that what you're doing?"

I shrug. It's uncomfortably close to the truth. "I'm aware that's how you get a village to accept you," I tell him.

"You don't think my sister publicly declaring you as her mate means the village will accept you? We respect the mating bond around here."

I shrug. I'm very sure the people around here don't want to upset Celia, but my goal is bigger than them just respecting my presence here.

Callum sets his bowl aside and actually sits down at the table like he's settling in for a long conversation. "The mating bond matters around here," he says slowly. "I know you didn't meet my parents, but if you had... you would understand."

There's a soft, mournful reverence in his voice when he talks about his parents and their bond. "You must miss them," I say, then wince. Absolutely nothing about Callum has indicated that he'd welcome my intrusion.

But he just nods. "I don't know how we go on without them," he admits quietly. "And I don't mean just us. Celia, she'll figure it out, but our parents—they were beloved. They were the foundation of our entire way of life. I don't think you understand how much we all relied on them." He gives me a sidelong look. "I know your pack didn't feel the same."

It feels like he wants to insult me a bit at the end, but I choose to ignore that and focus on his sincerity. I sit down, too, lowering my bowl and focusing entirely on him. "I have no opinion," I say as neutrally as I can. "I think you overestimate the vitriol of the average person in Stone Village. People like me just... existed. But I don't necessarily have a positive opinion either. I was trapped there. I didn't know anyone else."

I expect him to argue back. He's so angry, and I don't necessarily blame him. I don't think I'm a good target, but I respect that he doesn't have any others. The people who murdered his parents are out of his reach. The sister he's angry at is above reproach and out of his range, regardless. But I'm here.

It's not like I'm unfamiliar with being the person people take things out on. I can handle it.

He doesn't argue back, though. He just nods his head and fiddles with the bowl. "My parents mated centuries before I was born, but I've heard the stories," he says abruptly after a long minute. "And the way they ruled together, worked together—you don't have to worry about the people here not respecting you, Bethany. Trust me. People are just waiting for you and Celia to be like our parents."

That seems impossible, but I don't want to be the one to ruin his dreams. If he's coping with the loss by imagining a certain future, then I'll leave it to his siblings to ruin that for him. That's not my place.

"How's your dinner?"

"It's good. You have a talent for this," he admits.

"I'll make sure there's food for you here. But you should be home in time to eat it," I tell him.

I have no idea where he's going during the day, and I don't ask. This moment feels too fragile.

He nods. "I can do that. And I'll—I know you cleaned this entire place. I know the four of us let it go to shit after—well, after. And I know you've been chopping wood and gathering the food. I'll do my share again. Sorry."

It's as sweet as it is unexpected; I never thought a prince would say sorry for me taking care of domestic labor. I never thought he'd even notice.

My heart softens for him once more. Callum is winning me over slowly, inch by inch, moment by moment, revealing a hurt young man who just wants his life to go back to the way it was a few weeks ago or to at least have the opportunities to move forward that his siblings do.

His offer is the most tentative of peace offerings, but I accept it. Of course I do.

CHAPTER THIRTEEN

CELIA

No one seems happy when I announce that there's been a schedule change and we have to go back home for a night before moving forward, least of all me.

I need to start taking care of things, but unfortunately, I'm failing at even the most basic duties of my role. This is pure selfishness, but I can't resist it a moment longer.

This means my tour is going to take significantly longer, which leaves us vulnerable to the more resistant villages catching onto our weakness. They could align with Stone Village and mount an attack against us, all because I couldn't put my personal feelings aside and do my duty as queen to get the packs under control before my weaknesses get exposed.

Bryce is the only person who doesn't seem surprised or even judgmental. He just nods, then sends one of our guards ahead as a messenger, aiming to tell the next village that we'll be later than originally planned. He doesn't bother me as we ride back home. He doesn't dispute my excuse that it's to see if Heath returned with information, either, despite us both knowing that

Heath is very capable, but there's simply no way that he's already found the information we need.

A short trip. A night only. I just need... I don't know what I need, but even with the haze the moon puts on our minds, I can't forget her scent and her taste. It haunts me.

Maybe at home I can manage to sleep through the night.

***

When we arrive home, the hall is empty. It's not abandoned, at least—it's fresher and better kept than when we left—but neither Callum nor Bethany are here.

"Where have they gotten to?" I ask, agitation building up inside me. I somehow never expected them not to be waiting for me.

Bryce shrugs. "It's a big village, Celia. And we don't know your mate well yet. We don't know what she likes to do. She could be doing just about anything."

I don't think he means it as a condemnation of my skills as a mate, but it feels like one, anyway.

Bryce, much more capable of logic than me at this moment, finds someone walking past. "Have you seen them yet today?"

"Not Callum, but Bethany is with Agnes."

With Agnes? She's a nice woman who is closer to my parents' age, and I can't imagine what Bethany is doing with her. Still, it's a destination, so I turn away from the hall and start walking. "Celia, wait."

I stop just long enough to turn to Bryce. "Yes?"

"Don't you think you should let her have her space? Let her find her footing here?"

"I'm not stopping her," I tell him, already turning away from him.

"You're not helping her, either."

"If you have something to say, then say it."

He hurries to catch up to me. "Wait for her here. Maybe let's get a meal ready. We'll have dinner, the four of us. But let her find her place without you interfering."

"I'm not going to drag her away. I'm just... learning."

"This isn't a military campaign, Celia. She's not an enemy to study."

No, she's not, but I feel like I need to get the information, nonetheless. Who is this woman fate has bound me to? I should know her.

Bryce follows me as I continue to walk away. He doesn't have to if he's so uncomfortable with this. He could go find where our wayward little brother has gotten to. But he follows me, because that's all Bryce seems to do these days.

Bethany is fixing a chicken coop alongside Agnes, listening patiently as she's given instructions. I hold back and watch for a moment, seeing her work with sure, deft hands.

What is she doing out here? Why would she spend her time doing this?

Bethany, naturally, notices me first. She fumbles with the pegs she's holding, and her reaction makes Agnes look up at me and smile. "She's right helpful, this one," she says conspiratorially, like a meddling aunt thinking she's being a sneaky matchmaker.

We've already been matched, though. No one needs to force us in that regard.

"Is she," I say neutrally, but Agnes immediately starts nodding her head.

"Oh, yes. Chopping wood and cooking for everyone, and now she's here helping me with my chickens. Always helping someone out."

"Okay," Bethany interrupts, the first words she's said since I've arrived, and they're not even directed at me. "That's enough of that, Agnes. Should we get this done?" I've been dismissed. People don't dismiss me, not even before I was crowned. I'm a vital, central part of this pack. I'm welcome wherever I go. I don't get dismissed.

And I shouldn't get dismissed by my own mate.

But Agnes just waves Bethany off. "I can finish it. I've been taking care of this since long before you were born. Your mate is home. Go to her."

I'd give matchmaking aunts a pass if it weren't for the look Agnes gives me, moving her eyebrows in a way that is somehow utterly salacious.

Bethany hesitates for just a moment, but then hands the pins to Agnes and steps smartly out of the chicken coop. "Do you want your eggs now or later?" Agnes asks her.

"Later is fine," Bethany mutters, not looking at her. She's not looking at me, either, more staring at the ground.

I can feel Bryce's stare boring into my back. When I continue to ignore him, he sighs. "Let me help you finish that, Agnes," he offers.

"A fine idea," she agrees. "I'll have Bryce bring you your eggs, all right Bethany?"

"That's fine." She's still not looking at any of us.

"Shall we?" I offer her my arm, and after the briefest hesitation, she links her arm with mine, and we begin to walk away.

"Where's Callum?"

She tightens her grip on my arm, and then immediately releases it. "I have no idea."

"I thought I asked you to keep an eye on him."

"He's a grown man, Celia. He leaves in the morning and returns at night. I understand that that's pretty typical behavior for a grown man."

"He's twenty and he just lost his parents."

"Then maybe you should talk to him about that."

I take a deep breath, trying to control myself. I didn't come home to fight. But if we're mates, if this is going to work, if she's going to be by my side while I rule this pack, then she has to start acting like we're a team.

That brings me back to what I just saw and heard from Agnes. "So, you've been helping around the pack?"

"I understand that's how one acts in a pack."

It's like she's trying to spite me, remaining a blank wall as I'm trying to learn anything about her. "I suppose it is. I'm impressed you're working to fit in so quickly." She shrugs and doesn't offer me anything more. It's an infuriating lack of information. "Agnes said you've been chopping wood and cooking for people?"

"I already needed to cook for myself and Callum; I assumed I could cook for a few more. And as far as I know, the way to get what you need around here is to trade favors. Since I was left with nothing, I gave them what I knew how to do."

She starts walking a little faster, which would perhaps be an effective end to the conversation if her arm wasn't still through mine. I don't let her slip away. "I'm sorry. I thought, with Callum here..." That's just an excuse, though, and I think we both know it. The truth is I hadn't thought of it at all. I have a thousand excuses as to why that is—I've gone through a lot, I have bigger concerns, I have to worry about the whole pack, I assumed the pack would take care of her—but excuses aren't worth much.

She slows down when she realizes I won't let her go. "You can't have it both ways, Celia," she says, voice soft again. "Either Callum needs me to look out for him, or he was capable of ensuring the two of us are taken care of. Choose one."

It's perhaps a valid criticism, but it hurts to hear it from her in a way that it doesn't from anyone else. "I'm only home for one day," I tell her, side-stepping her response. "Could we just... not argue? I have to leave again tomorrow."

She's quiet for a long moment, but then nods. "All right. Let's go back to the hall, then. If you're here, and Bryce is here, and Callum will presumably show back up later... I need to start dinner sooner rather than later."

It feels like a hollow victory, but she doesn't let go of my arm, so I take what I can get.

Chapter Fourteen

Bethany

I could cut the tension in the hall with the same knife I used to prepare dinner. It's so heavy and thick between the four of us that I'm surprised it can't be physically seen.

Callum refuses to answer his sister's questions about where he's been, telling her "out" sullenly and then giving her the silent treatment when she presses. Bryce just watches all three of us like he's trying to solve something particularly complex, and Celia retreats inward when it becomes clear she's getting nowhere with Callum.

At least Bryce remembered to bring the eggs. They're the only way to stretch dinner far enough to feed all four of us.

In Stone Village, I'd cook along with the others at the bottom of the pack hierarchy. We'd labor over the food, often spending the better part of the day preparing it, but we'd always eat last and get the smallest portions of whatever remained. In contrast, Bryce had gestured gracefully for me to eat first, and neither Celia nor Callum had contradicted him, so I'd served myself a modest portion before ensuring everyone else got enough.

It's nice to know that things are different here. That I'm not going to be given the scraps. I'm given a place at their table and a meal equal to theirs. Still, it's hard to ignore that I prepared the meal and now I have to sit here while they all look like they're slowly being petrified to stone around the table.

"Thank you," Bryce remembers to say when he finishes, and I give a nod.

Calum pushes back from the table as soon as he says that, like Bryce's words are the release he's been waiting for. He walks right out the door, and Celia half-rises to follow him.

Bryce sighs. "Let him go. He's clearly not leaving, and it doesn't seem like he's getting in any real trouble."

Celia runs a hand through her short hair. "Shouldn't he have outgrown this stage already? He's twenty."

"He's young. And not wanting to be at home—especially given the things that have happened recently—is normal," I interject, the first thing I've said in too long.

The silence hangs heavy, the reminder of what happened to their parents once again appearing like a specter, and I hate myself for saying it even as I felt compelled to defend Callum. Just one more reason for them to despise me and everyone I know.

"I'll talk to him," Bryce offers after a long moment, and Celia gives him a disbelieving look. "Well, you're not getting through to him."

"He needs to learn to do better," she says. "He doesn't have to like it, but he does have to listen." I shiver despite the fire being well-fed. The cold in her tone is brutal.

I can't help but notice Bryce darting a look at me, but he keeps speaking anyway, clearly deciding that I deserve to hear whatever is going on. I wonder if that means he considers me part of the family now, or if it's just more inconvenient to tell me to leave. "You gave Heath and me roles, Celia. I know he's young, but he's floundering."

"He is young," she says with finality. She hesitates a moment, then admits, "We just lost our parents. Don't ask me to lose him too. He's not ready for any of this."

I bite my tongue to keep from offering my opinion.

Bryce just looks at her. "I'll talk to him," is all he says.

When it's clear that they're not going to say any more, I interrupt. "I can clean now, or I can get out of the way and clean in the morning. Whatever will be the least intrusive."

Bryce looks thoughtful for a minute, then says, "You know what? Leave it for Callum and me. Maybe he really just does need something to do."

Asking him to come home and clean a house when it's obvious that he wants to be doing the same level of tasks as his brothers seems like a recipe for disaster, but no one asked my opinion. I just nod and go to retreat.

Footsteps echo behind me, and I stop. Right, it's Celia's bedroom. Should I go and sleep somewhere else?

"You've been staying here?" she asks. I nod. "Good. Let's go."

Bemused, I follow her inside and watch her pull off her clothes. Far from being sexual, she does it with the practicality of a soldier after a long day. She immediately slides into bed, pulling a blanket around her.

I stand awkwardly for a moment, unsure where she wants me or what she expects of me. "Well? Are you coming?" She interrupts my train of thought.

I don't take off all my clothes. I shed my outer layer, then slide into the bed beside her and close my eyes while she wraps an arm around me.

***

I wake up in the middle of the night sweating buckets.

I should have expected that. I should have remembered that, even though I've been cold, I'm now sharing a bed with a proper, full-blooded wolf and that Celia radiates heat.

I try to be quiet when I climb out of bed, but Celia is awake in an instant. "What's wrong?"

"Too hot."

"Too many layers," she agrees, watching me intently. Her eyes are still alert even as she lets her body relax and sinks back into bed.

She won't look away from me, so I strip down even with her watching, turning my head partially away so I don't have to watch her, too. I try to keep the same brisk, practical mentality she had earlier, but I'm not sure how well I succeed.

I'm naked now, and I'm trying not to let it get to me, trying to tell my body that we are not naked because our mate is here and we want to start something. This is merely practicality. That's all. Nothing more.

"Sleep," Celia demands. "I need sleep."

I slide back into bed. I foolishly think the blanket will hide it all, erasing the awkwardness of the last moment, but then I feel her warm skin slide against mine, ruining that thought. She's so soft. Her muscles are firm and strong, but her skin and the fine, downy hair on it is the softest, most gentle thing I've ever touched.

Her arm bands across me, pulling me where she wants me, and I'm hyper-aware of her touch on my stomach, inches from my breasts. I hold my breath while she moves me around to where she wants me, pulling me closer to her, pressing our bodies skin to skin.

But then I feel her soft breaths on my neck, and Celia is entirely asleep again, her nose buried in my hair as her grip around me relaxes completely.

***

When I wake up, I'm alone.

The bed is still warm, so I probably haven't been alone for long. I scramble out of the blankets and find my underdress. Then, instead of messing about with more layers, I simply pull the blanket around me and go to look for Celia.

Callum sits glumly at the table, eyes focused intently on the wood grain like he's learning the secrets of the universe from that spot. "You missed them," he says. "Just missed them. You might still be able to see them."

I shouldn't, but I can't help myself as I run to the door, throwing it open. Sure enough, I can see their backs on horseback as they go up the hill, once more leaving us behind.

Chapter Fifteen

Celia

Bryce is giving me the silent treatment.

He follows orders when I give them, not questioning me when I say it's time to go. But he's making it clear that he's not happy about it.

Still, I'm significantly better rested now, which means I'm prepared to hold my tongue. Bryce can think what he wants. He doesn't get a say in how I handle this.

And he should be glad to be back to business. Isn't helping me secure the packs his primary purpose?

Whether or not he's prepared to do it, I need to turn my attention fully to pack business. My job now is to make it clear that it's in everyone's best interest to follow the Crae line as they have since before recorded history. My job is to show them that we are firm and strong and can still protect them as we always have.

"Any advice for today?" I ask Bryce as we get closer to our destination.

He's quiet for a long moment. Just when I think he is seriously imma-ture enough to give me the silent treatment, he speaks. "The people need reassurance, Celia."

"I know that."

"Then give them to them."

It's advice a toddler could have given, and somehow it's all Bryce has to say. I suppose this is his first time in this role, too, although I expected someone who sat at our parents' sides for so long to do better.

***

This village is geographically the second furthest away from ours. The only one further is Stone Village, but that's in the complete opposite direction, with ours in the middle.

This is a small village. A lot of them are—history tells us that they started off as a few individual families, back when werewolves were more prone to dens than homes and halls. Then, a few generations later, the few families would band together for resources, creating the little villages we know today.

This village is particularly small, though, with just ten homes scattered around. They do everything communally, which explains the four children running around with limited supervision as we all sit and talk by the fire.

"I want to be honest," Brash, the de facto leader of this village, says, "We've already had a man from Stone Village come through here."

I shouldn't be surprised, but I somehow am, my stomach lurching uncomfortably. "What did they offer you?"

"Food," his daughter pipes up. I'm mildly embarrassed that I don't remember her name. "Resources to get through cold winters and long sum-mers. We do okay up here, but I can't deny that the offer of more is a compelling one."

"Was anyone tempted?" Bryce asks slowly while my mind is stuck on what Ames is offering people.

It's the same as the last village. Resources. They're stolen, and we all know it; Ames has no compunctions about killing people to take what he wants. He might provide resources, but they'll be as blood-soaked as everything else he touches.

"By what promises to be a war? No. We just hope one doesn't show up at our hearth anyway," Brash says. His voice is carefully neutral, but I can't pretend that he's not staring intently at me as I sit by his hearth.

"No one wants war," Bryce says for me.

"No one ever wants war. And yet..." The daughter shakes her head, then turns to look over the children as if compulsively checking. "That said, if Stone Village is going around pack to pack, and if you're chasing them, it's going to make travel difficult. And we need to be able to travel."

Small packs travel between villages to trade whatever they have. Young wolves coming of age travel when they're looking for a mate or even a temporary partner they haven't known since birth. I can understand her concern.

"We'll resolve the problem. In the meantime, don't entertain them here. Turn them away."

Brash sucks his teeth. "They turn up armed, you know."

"You think I don't know?" I challenge, and the air hangs heavy. I know. My parents found out the hard way. I'm here because of it.

We all know it, and I don't retract my order to not shelter them here. Everyone stares at me for a moment, and I purposefully avoid blinking, staring everyone down so they get my point.

***

"What exactly gave you the impression that asking them to put their lives on the line for you was the way to win their loyalty?" Bryce demands testily once we're alone. "It's supposed to be the other way around, Celia. Loyalty first. Then people will die for you."

"I didn't ask them to go to war. Just not to harbor enemies of the crown."

"You asked them to stand up against trained soldiers. Trained soldiers who killed our parents, both very competent fighters. Most of these people are farmers, Celia."

When Bryce gets worked up like this, he doesn't get loud. His voice gets deeper, his eyes more intense, and there's a certain stillness to him that's more frightening than shouting would be. He reminds me of our father, and this dressing down feels like being scolded as a child again. "Don't lecture me, Bryce."

I had to take lectures from our father. That was expected, and he made me who I needed to be. I don't have to take anything of the sort from Bryce.

"Someone needs to. Would you prefer to hear it from Heath? He'd tell you the same. This is how you lose people. Either their lives or their loyalty; apparently, you're not picky."

That is a slap in the face. The idea that anyone would ever believe I don't care about the lives of the wolves under my command guts me. "I am trying to save the wolves," I remind him, forcing myself to keep calm.

He gives me a raised eyebrow and a judgmental look. "Look, if you want to save the wolves, ignore Stone Village. Listen to what else they're telling you. I know you're focused on Ames because he's a threat, and that makes sense. But Heath is getting you the information you need. For now, focus on what will actually inspire loyalty among these packs. If they need resources—"

"We're done talking about this," I say. I know I'm being short with him, but what else can I do? I can't have him thinking that this type of thing is okay. We're not here to endlessly debate and manage what I say. This crown is on my head, and now I have to decide how best to wield it.

And right now, the biggest danger to all wolves is Stone Village. I'll do whatever it takes to keep them from growing a bigger foothold in any of the packs.

"Fine," Bryce says cooly, turning away from me, apparently ready to be done as well. "But I won't take it back, Celia."

I know he won't. If there's one thing us Crae siblings are good at, it's being stubborn.

Well, too bad for him. He can be as stubborn as he wants, but one of us has been appointed to make the final decision, and it's not him.

CHAPTER SIXTEEN

BETHANY

Callum comes home quietly, clearly expecting me to be asleep.

I appreciate the respect of not wanting to wake me up, but unfortunately, I'm not asleep. The bed feels all wrong without Celia in it, and I had tossed and turned for what felt like forever before admitting defeat and getting up to get some work done.

I thought perhaps I could exhaust myself into being tired, but all I've done is knead plenty of bread and clean the entire house.

He blinks and looks at me. He's half-covered in mud, and I wish he wouldn't come home like this, but I don't say anything as he just stares. "You're awake."

"So are you."

He rolls his eyes. "Yes, I'm awake. Obviously. But you're not usually by now."

I huff a laugh. "Callum, you've only known me a few days. You have no idea what's usual for me."

"Someone's snappish tonight."

Am I? I don't think that's especially snappish, but then again, Callum is used to me being as unobtrusive as possible, so perhaps the contrast is startling.

My mate came home yesterday to be critical and cold, then held me in the softest, sweetest embrace only to leave at dawn. I think I'm justified in not being at my best.

I sigh and sit down at the table, letting my tired muscles relax for a moment. "Where have you been all day, anyway?" I turn the tables. "Hm? Your siblings wanted to know—did Bryce get the answer out of you?"

"It's none of Bryce's business. Not yours, either."

He's not wrong. And before tonight, I haven't truly cared, either. Callum is an adult and practically a stranger to me; what he does with his time is no one's concern but his own. Even so, I don't let it go. "I'm asking anyway."

He grits his teeth, then slides into the chair opposite mine, dirt-crusted clothes no doubt staining the recently cleaned chairs. "My parents stopped supporting a standing army. Said we were safe out here, that no one would come after the wolves. It's one of the reasons we were susceptible to attack. I'm trying to rectify that."

"And you're organizing it? Training people?" I ask, trying to keep the skepticism from my voice.

"I'm trying to."

"You're not fully grown yet, Callum. You're not fully immortal yet, are you?"

"No. Still a few years away, probably." I look him over. Judging by his brothers, he's more like ten years away. Which means that any training he's doing right now could be incredibly dangerous; a knife wound for someone as young as him won't heal in a few minutes. It could even technically be fatal.

It's not common, but I doubt that matters. Celia asked me to look after him, and I defended him doing whatever he wished. Now, I'm learning that he's going off to play soldier with his still-breakable body.

He rolls his eyes. "I'm a fully trained soldier, Bethany. You think the prince of wolves could grow up without learning how to defend himself? Each and every one of my siblings knocked me around until I could push back. I'm capable of this."

"And if you get hurt?"

"Better than getting dead in another attack from Stone Village, wouldn't you say?"

He's not wrong about that. Ames won't care that he's only twenty. Ames will run him through in his attempt to get one step closer to power. And he'll have to, won't he? Callum is in line for the throne, and Ames will have to eliminate Celia and all the heirs to have his way.

A spike of fear stabs me in the heart. It physically hurts to think of Ames coming after these people. I don't even know them yet. I can't lie and say I truly care about them. But I don't want them to be hurt.

Callum's young, but his assessment of the situation is incredibly accurate. He's risking a little pain now against the very real and serious risk of death later. I can't say I blame him.

"Would you teach me?" I ask after a long moment.

He startles, clearly not expecting that. "What?"

"I asked if you'd teach me," I say, speaking up more clearly. When he continues to look at me like I'm speaking a foreign tongue, I smile. "What, you expected a lecture?"

"Yes," he says simply. "That tends to be how it goes. Why do you want to learn?"

"Ames is coming for us all," I point out. "And I'm your sister's mate."

He studies me for a long moment, then nods slowly. "I think I can work something out," he muses. "It would have to be after regular training."

"Why?"

"Because you're not becoming a soldier, Bethany."

I shrug. "I could."

"Do you even know what it means to be a soldier?"

Do you? I want to ask, but I refrain. "I want the training," I say instead of debating with him. "I'll tell you if it's too much."

He looks at me for a long minute, taking my measure, judging my worth. I force myself to hold still and let him look. At last, he nods. "We start at dawn."

Him giving in without argument gives me the courage to say what I have to admit. Celia had asked and I hadn't told her, but Callum needs to know if we're going to do this. And maybe, if we both know each other's secrets, then it'll be a little more fair.

"One thing you should know before we start," I say, "I'm nearly as fragile as you are."

He goes very still. "What does that mean?"

"Exactly what it sounds like. I'm immortal, but I break a little easier. Take a little longer to heal. I'm not quite as invulnerable as you're used to."

"Half-human," he mutters, understanding lighting his eyes.

"Yeah. Is that a problem?" I tilt my chin up, phrasing it as a clear challenge.

He studies me for a long moment, and I know he wants to call the whole thing off. But, to his credit, he doesn't. "I can work with that," he says gruffly before getting out of his chair and stalking off to his bedroom.

***

We're both up before dawn. Thankfully, I prepared so much bread last night that we have food before Callum leads the way to the clearing away from the village, where a dozen or so wolves are waiting for us.

"Not bad," he mumbles. When he sees me looking, he clarifies. "Not everyone can be spared from work at home every day. People come when they can. That's not how a standing army should work, but what can you do? People need to eat."

I don't know what I expected, but this is not that. Callum doesn't give any speeches or even any orders. Members of the gathering begin to pair off once we arrive, weapons already in hand. They're truly preparing for war by beating the shit out of each other.

Callum doesn't spare me another glance. "Honor."

A female wolf trots up to his side. "Yes?"

"Show Bethany the basics today."

Honor looks me up and down. "No weapon?"

"Start smaller," he says over his shoulder, already hoisting his sword and heading into a fight.

I'm a little stung that he won't even work with me, but I try my best to let it go and give Honor my full attention. "What does start smaller mean?"

"It means you need to start with footwork. How to stand, how to move. How to fall," she says absently, like she's making the list more for herself than for me. "The very basics."

I shrug; that sounds accurate to me.

"Shall we begin?"

CHAPTER SEVENTEEN

BETHANY

Honor is a punishing taskmaster. I think half my body is a bruise, and she never even raises a hand to me, never mind a weapon. But she demands excellence, forcing me to hold stances until she deems them accurate. Then she moves on to ensuring that I know how to fall properly. She says no one can learn to fight without knowing how to fall, which results in me falling on the ground a few hundred times.

I see how Callum comes home so covered in dirt every day.

When we trudge in the front door of the hall, Callum stops short. "Forgot it wouldn't smell good today," he mutters.

My heart warms slightly. In such a short time, he's gotten used to my cooking and has come to rely on it. "Not today," I say with as much cheer as I can muster after a punishing day. "There's bread, though."

He frowns, and I know bread isn't enough for a growing werewolf who was physically active all day. But there's nothing I can do about that. "I'm going to take a bath," I tell him. "Leave something for me."

***

The river is ice cold, which is honestly perfect after the hot work of the day. I jump in with my dress still on, stained and ruined as it is, then strip it off once it's soaked so I can scrub it and my skin. The moon is the only one to watch me as I bathe in the frigid water.

Today felt good. Today felt different from anything I've ever known. I'm not deluded into thinking I'm in any way capable of defending myself yet, but this is one step closer.

I came here to defend myself and my mother, and I thought I'd need to do so by serving my way into a position where they'd want to protect me. But the idea that I could simply protect myself never crossed my mind.

I have bruises, but I'm not worried about them. They'll fade soon enough, and they don't even hurt that bad. And if this is the cost of giving myself the future I need—a future free of Ames, a future with a home and my mother and where I know I'm safe, finally—then I'll happily pay it.

***

By the time the sun is high in the sky the next day, I regret the wasted time in the bath when I could have been sleeping. Not that I slept especially well when I got back to the hall, but it's the principle of the thing—I feel like I can use all the rest possible right now as Honor knocks me into the dirt again.

And again, and again. She's testing my footwork from yesterday, seeing how stable I am on my feet. I still haven't been given a weapon, and I don't think that'll happen for a while yet, judging by the way I'm clearly failing her test.

She helps me up again, giving my hand a squeeze. "Need a rest?"

"No, I'm fine. Keep going."

"It's not a failure to rest," she says firmly.

I look around the training ground, where people very clearly are not resting. I highly doubt the word is in the vocabulary of anyone here.

"You'll burn out if you don't." I don't respond to that, unwilling to explain why I need to work harder than anyone else.

But maybe Honor has already figured some of it out on her own, because she doesn't press it any further. "One thing you need is better clothes," she muses. "Could your mate lend you something?"

"She's bigger than me," I point out, which seems like a logical concern. I'm certainly not going to tell Honor that Celia hardly gave me permission to sleep in her bed, never mind to wear her clothes.

"True. Let me see what I can do tonight," she says, eyeing me carefully like she's taking my measurements. "For now—get water. Then come back."

"Yes, ma'am," I mutter, but I can't say I'm not grateful for the momentary break.

Callum joins me at the water bucket someone filled this morning. "Are you okay?" he asks quietly.

"I'm fine. Why would I not be fine?"

He shrugs. "You're falling a lot. It's not unusual, but you told me about your condition, and I—"

I turn to face him fully. "Let's get one thing straight, Callum. I'm not more fragile than you are. In fact, I'm less fragile, because I still heal faster than a mortal. So things take me a little more effort. The cost can be a little more physical. You're playing around with swords where one good stab could kill you, and you're the heir to this pack. So don't say anything to me."

He raises an eyebrow. "First of all, I'm third in line, so me being an heir is irrelevant. Second, I got all of my clumsy, falling stages out of the way a decade ago, so I'm not worried about my own body. I'm asking if you're okay, Bethany."

He is, I realize belatedly. He just wants to know if I'm okay. Sullen, rude Callum has practically disappeared now that I know his secret and haven't tried to stop him. He's earnest, and for the first time, I see a future leader shining out from the angry kid.

"I'll be fine. This is how you learn. Nothing worth doing ever came without a little pain."

"Speaking from experience?"

"Absolutely. Now, Honor is waiting for me, so..."

He gestures back toward the training field. "Don't let me stop you, then." He hesitates a moment, then says, "Actually, first, I have a question."

I stop. "Go ahead."

"There was only bread again this morning."

"That's not a question." It's not, but I know what he means to say. There was only bread. I should have provided more. I wonder if I can work through the night—it's not like I'm sleeping much anyway—or if he's going to force me to cut back on the training.

"And I realized how much you've been doing. The four of us never worked out how we'd keep the house running just us, and then they left without a plan."

I bite my lip to say that Celia at least had clearly had a plan, and it had been for me to care for Callum. I'd like to think that shows a level of trust that only mates can have. I worry that it shows that she's using me, just like everyone else I've ever known.

"So I was thinking... I don't know how to do what you do. But show me, and you and I can make a plan to split the chores. At least until the other three come back, and then we can make a plan for the five of us to split them."

It's so unexpected that I can't believe I've heard him right. "You're going to sweep mud off the floor?" I challenge.

He shrugs. "If that's what needs to be done."

"It does. You track in more mud than anyone I've ever met."

He has the grace to look abashed. "Then I'll start there. If you show me how to cook, we can share that, too."

He's radiating sincerity even as I can't quite believe he means it. I guess we'll find out later tonight. "Sure. We'll figure it out tonight. But if you want to eat something besides bread, we can't stay here until the middle of the night."

He looks up at the sky, already well past the midday point, and sighs. "Then we better train fast," he mutters, and now I feel that he and I are completely on the same page.

CHAPTER EIGHTEEN

CELIA

I manage to avoid going home for over a week. One long, miserable week.

Bryce won't even talk to me when he doesn't need to anymore. I haven't slept. I see my failures in the eyes of every villager we speak with.

Queens should be trained during peacetime, given the room and grace to make mistakes when lives don't depend on the decisions we make. Unfortunately, it rarely works out that way. Power somehow never transitions peacefully.

I swallow. Is that the fate that awaits me someday? To die bloody and leave one of my siblings, or even one of our children, struggling to learn what to do when the crown is placed on their head?

My thoughts are consumed by a bloody future and the sinking feeling that it might not be that far away. What is the shortest reign a wolf queen has ever had? If I'm not careful, that could be my future.

"We should go see if Heath is back yet," I tell Bryce. We've been riding in painful silence for an hour. Bryce is not known for being especially chatty, and yet this isn't like any other silence between us. This silence is painful and biting.

Bryce remains quiet for another moment. At last, he simply says, "Okay," and I can't tell if he agrees with me or just doesn't want to argue anymore.

"And we should check on Callum," I add, just to incentivize him further. We've both been worried about Callum, who's gone through two decades of life without keeping secrets but is suddenly sneaking around behind our backs and refusing to reveal where he's spending his time. He picked the worst time to go through a rebellious phase.

Maybe Heath will be back, and then I can make Callum his problem. It's obvious that Bethany isn't up for it, and Callum has always been closest to Heath.

Why couldn't he have gotten this out of his system a year ago?

"We should," Bryce says, wrinkling his brow. The mention of Callum clears the air between us, and suddenly, we are who we were before: two siblings looking out for our family. "I'm worried about him."

"Me too."

"I'm sure Bethany is looking out for him," he says reassuringly.

"I'm sure she's doing what she can," I say, and I don't mean to sound dismissive, but I'm sure I do. I don't mean to. Bethany seems to be a good person, and I have faith that she means well, but I have less faith that she'll be successful. It's not a criticism of her; I've seen her try to integrate with the pack, and that's a wonderful thing. It speaks to her working to be successful as my mate. But Callum is a prince of the realm, and Bethany has already admitted she's not trying to keep him in check at all. She's too used to serving people to actually put her foot down.

No, it needs to be one of us there for him. And I can't spare Bryce, as much as he's annoying me now, so I'm hoping Heath will be prepared to step into the job.

Bryce opens his mouth, but I don't want his opinion on how I feel about my mate, so I cut him off. "Let's move," I say shortly. "The sooner we're home, the sooner we can know what needs to be done."

***

When we get close to the village, I don't bother going to the hall. I learned my lesson last time. Instead, I follow my nose, looking for Bethany's clean, fresh berry scent.

Bizarrely, the scent leads us right out of the village proper. Last time I was here, Agnes said she was chopping wood for multiple pack members, but we're further out of the way than she'd need to go for that. Did she get lost? That shouldn't be possible for a wolf, but I still remember that she refused to tell me how being half-human affects her, and I urge my horse faster.

I can hear them before I see them, the sounds of fighting distinctive and unmistakable. My muscles lock, ready for a fight, ready for some sort of battle. We didn't expect Stone Village to be so brazen to attack our village again, but here they are, and—

And Callum is the one with a sword held to my mate's neck. My heart is in my throat, unable to look away, unable to fully process what I'm seeing.

Bethany stares him down, and then she swings at him. Callum, to my surprise, holds still for a long moment, waiting until the last possible second to dodge out of the way. Then, in a clearly telegraphed move, he sweeps her legs and takes her to the ground.

She huffs when she lands, then lies very still for a moment. That breaks my paralysis, and I rush forward. "What the fuck is going on here?" I demand of no one in particular.

Callum huffs. "Hi to you too, sister."

"What the fuck is going on?" I repeat, willing anyone to answer my question.

It's Bethany, still lying on the ground, who answers me. "We're training."

"Training?" I echo.

"Training," Callum confirms, and he gets a firm set on his face. "You thought that, after everything, we wouldn't want to be prepared?"

"And what's she doing here?" I demand, gesturing to my mate. "Hm?"

"You don't think I also need to know how to defend myself?" Bethany asks. She's still lying on the ground, and it hasn't escaped my notice that she hasn't even tried to get up. Callum steps into her space and extends a hand, and I have to bite back a growl.

I shouldn't be letting instinct drive me like this. I shouldn't feel so close to demanding Callum fight me himself over him touching her hand.

Thankfully, I restrain myself. When she's back on her feet, Bethany shakes herself out a bit, her attention on Callum and not me, testing my already weak restraint. "That was better," he tells her. "You're still taking too long to decide. Decide, commit, act. You can't debate."

She nods seriously, stepping back into a prepared stance without him even asking. Bryce steps up next to me like he's going to personally stop me from doing something stupid.

His presence is a good reminder of how many people are watching, and I force myself to take a few deep breaths. I can keep myself in check. This is my little brother with my mate; he's not doing anything inappropriate. He's teaching her to defend herself.

Bethany swings first, a little wild and too wide, wasting precious energy. Callum doesn't correct her, just stepping out of the way. He barely needs to move around the wide swing, but he makes his step obvious, regardless.

I've never seen Callum teach before. I helped train him myself—we all did. He's recently grown into his body, and his size and confidence have made him a formidable appointment. I know he could probably take on all of us and win, but I somehow never stopped seeing him as the little boy I trained.

But not anymore. Callum might still be young, and might have years to go before he reaches his immortality, but no one can call him a child anymore. Not even me.

He dodges another clumsy strike, then another before he's apparently done playing with Bethany and strikes back. The flat of his blade hits her right across the sternum, sending her sprawling to the dirt.

And I see red.

There is no more room in my mind for rational thought or reason. I draw my own weapon before I even fully process what I'm doing, already advancing on my brother. Caught off guard, he's not ready for me, and he barely dodges my first attack.

This isn't the slow, cautious fight of a few moments ago. I swing with force and determination. I have enough restraint not to go for the neck, but other than that, I'm aiming to hurt.

Callum blocks each blow. "What the fuck, Celia?"

I can't make the words come. Instead, I bare my teeth at him and swing again and again and again.

And I get nowhere. Callum is even better than I thought he was, blocking expertly as he weaves around me. He doesn't strike back, either, just waiting for me to come to my senses.

It's all the eyes that I can feel watching us that force me to re-evaluate. I'm irrational and feel closer to my wolf than I ever have before, but the part of me that's trained since birth to be a queen recognizes the dangerous situation. A queen doesn't lose her shit. And our family can never afford to show in-fighting.

I step back and lower my weapon. Callum does the same, eyeing me like a rabid dog who will strike again without warning.

I take deep, heaving breaths, and my lungs are filled with the berry-fresh scent of my mate. I'm okay. It's okay. We're okay.

Bryce steps up beside Callum, as if he thinks he needs to defend him from me. Didn't he just see the way he fights? Callum might still be young, but apparently he's not a child anymore.

With one last look at me, Callum ignores both of us and turns his attention to Bethany. "Better job committing that time. Next time, we'll work on controlling your swings."

I stop watching my brother, confident that he won't hurt me, and turn my attention to Bethany. She's on her feet now, and she's listening to Callum with rapt attention.

"Not today," I say shortly, and I stride over to take her arm to escort her away. Surely, no one can judge me for this. Surely, everyone understands that I'm doing what I can to hold on to the last thread of rationality.

Bethany has the grace to walk with me and match my frantic stride until we're out of sight, and then she wretches her arm from my grip. I let her go immediately, never intending to hurt her or drag her around, but I immediately feel somehow bereft without her. I take a step closer as if compelled to, and to my frustration, she takes a step back.

"What the fuck was that?" she demands. She keeps her voice low, likely in deference to not knowing how close any other wolves are, but the cold menace in her voice could be heard on the other side of the mountain. "Celia, what the fuck?"

I shrug. "I saw someone hurt my mate. You can't blame me."

"You know full well I asked for it. I was there by choice. I'm learning."

"And are you going to join Callum's little band of soldiers?" I ask with more heat in my voice than I intend to, but I can't help it. The thought of her as a soldier on the front line of battle makes my blood boil with pain.

I haven't even begun to think about Callum and his band of soldiers. An army not summoned by the queen is a huge problem, and I'll need to handle them soon. Maybe Bryce is already laying into Callum for me, but I doubt that will be the end of it. Callum is just as stubborn as the rest of us.

But that's a problem for later. Right now, I need to get the image of Bethany fighting for her life out of my head.

"I'd like to survive if there's an attack," she snaps back, and the air around us goes eerily still. We both know what she's referring to.

"They were better trained than you'll probably ever be," I say with a heavy voice as I think about my parent's bodies. "And they couldn't survive."

"So, what, we should lay down and die?" she demands. "Accept defeat now? I didn't think you believed in that. I thought you'd fight, Celia. Isn't that what you've been doing?"

Is it? I've certainly said things about winning against Ames and Stone Village and ensuring stability returns to the wolves. But I don't have any more of a plan now than I did at the funeral.

My little brother has more of a plan. It's a terrible plan, but it's still more than I have.

I'm not going to tell her that, though; that's a weakness I can't afford.

"There's plenty of people to keep you safe."

"Yes, Callum and his soldiers. And you, if you're here."

If you're here shouldn't hurt like it does. I'm not abandoning her or running off with no real purpose. I'm leaving because it's my job, and because it's what the wolves need me to do. Even so, it cuts when she says it.

I step toward her again, and this time, she doesn't back away. I take her shoulders in a grip as gentle as I can make it. "I promise you, Bethany. I'm going to take care of this, all right? That's my job. I'll take care of Stone Village and the threat will be over. You'll be safe. Everyone will be safe."

She stares at me for a long moment, then gives me a slow smile. "You know, I think that's the sweetest thing you've said to me so far."

"Yeah?" She's probably not wrong, and I know that's not fair to her. I'll be sweet later. We both know there are more pressing concerns than me being sweet right now.

She gives me a nod. "It doesn't mean I'm giving up training with Callum."

I frown at her, but she has a stubborn set to her eyes. It's different from mine and my brother's. Her stubbornness isn't quite a brick wall. It's a strong plant stalk, flexible and bending, yet still unyielding to pressure. It's as immovable as mine in her own way.

"All right, then." I look her over, covered in dirt. Clearly, she was knocked to the ground more than the two times I witnessed today. "Want a bath?"

She raises an eyebrow. "Are you offering to join me?"

I nod, finding myself inexplicably bashful. I'm not a bashful person, but here I am with butterflies in my stomach just looking at her.

But all she does is give me a smile. "I'd like that."

Chapter Nineteen

Bethany

The river is freezing. I doubt Celia truly notices, but I do, and I have to fight not to show it. It won't be a very good romantic moment if my teeth are chattering, after all.

And I can feel that's what this is. It's a romantic moment, and whether or not it's just a release of Celia's tension again or an overture to starting over, I find that I can't make myself care. I want this. No, I need this.

I do have plenty of dirt on me, so I jump in with the clothes Honor found me, then take them off so I can scrub them while I'm also getting clean. Celia doesn't seem worried about her own clothes, although they smell like horse. She strips quickly and leaves them in a pile on the bank, striding into the water like she's not providing a view that makes my mouth water.

I never thought strong thighs were a thing that I was so attracted to, but I can't stop staring. I know from when she held me in bed that the skin is soft, but the muscles beneath that skin bunch and move as she walks, showing sheer power.

And the sweet, pretty sex between them, barely hidden behind dark curls—I haven't tasted her since the full moon. I want to taste her again.

Celia smiles at me when she notices I've been watching, but instead of doing anything about it, she just lies back, letting the water hold her weight. Rather than distracting me, this enhances the view, her whole toned, strong body on display for my perusal.

I saw her under the full moon, but that hardly counts. And when we slept in her bed, I felt her, but I barely saw her.

But now, I can look to my heart's content. The cold water makes her dusky nipples harden, the only sign that she feels cold at all, and I want to suck one. Would she like that?

It's like instincts have taken over, because I have no idea how to do any of this. I don't know how to please a mate; I barely know what mates do together.

"Are you going to touch, or just look?"

"Well, now that I know I'm invited..." I say, and I mean for it to sound teasing, but I fear that I don't succeed. She doesn't ever need to let me touch her, of course. But the cold distance between us has been a sharp, caustic thing, and I didn't want to overstep and upset her.

She hasn't even opened her eyes, reclining in the cold water like it's the warmest bath. "You're invited. If you want."

Do I detect hesitation from her, too? Could we both be feeling a little unsure? Celia always seems so certain, so decided. She reeks of confidence and never hesitates in any of her decisions. Perhaps I'm just wishing she feels like I do.

But I don't question her offer, instead walking closer to her until I'm right next to her. Her eyes are still closed as she floats there, and I trail my hand along her exposed stomach. She pushes into my touch, and my blood heats.

I trail my hand up to her breast, cupping the small mound and squeezing it slightly. Celia gasps, and then she's on her feet, moving toward me. She uses two fingers to tilt my chin up, and her eyes are a smoldering void that I can't look away from. Usually so bright and gold, there's a dark intensity to them now. "Tell me you want this," she says, her voice as dark as her eyes.

"I want this."

"Tell me I can touch you."

"Please."

She smiles, slow and like some sort of violent beast that plans to eat me up. "All right then," she murmurs, and she's kissing me before I can respond.

The kiss is hungry, and she bites her way into my mouth, still holding my chin like she's afraid I'll run away. "Off," she mumbles after a moment, her breath sending warm little puffs against my chilled skin as she says it. She tugs on my clothes to make it perfectly clear. "You're still too dressed."

She helps me peel the sopping wet fabric off, and rather than washing it like I originally planned, we hurl it onto the shore, bunched up and no doubt only growing filthier. I can't find it in myself to care, not when Celia is already kissing me like her life depends on it once more.

"Shore?" I ask, panting slightly from the force of her kiss.

Celia's already shaking her head. "Right here." She grabs my hips to adjust me like she wants and then moves her thigh until it's pressing between my legs. I moan at the contact and Celia smiles wickedly. "Ride my thigh, sweetheart. Make your pretty cunt come."

I feel feverish, a bizarre contradiction to the cool water, but with help from her insistent hands, I begin to ride her thigh, finding the right angle to rock at until the pressure is building inside me until everything is tingling and I'm worried I'll die if I don't get relief.

"That's it," Celia murmurs. "Make yourself feel good."

I already feel so good, but I'm hungry for more, grinding a little harder against her thigh, searching for it. I need this, need just a little more, and—

The pleasure is overwhelming, spreading through my body as I lock her thigh in place between mine and ride out the orgasm. I don't remember ever being cold because my veins are filled with fire as I rock against her. Godsdamn, I didn't realize it would feel this good.

Celia strokes my hair as I come down from my high, then slowly lowers her thigh away. I whimper, bereft at the loss while simultaneously glad for the time to recover.

"That was beautiful," she murmurs. "So fucking pretty for me."

My hips rock against nothing but river water in response to that.

"Your turn," I say with as much firmness as I can muster, despite the fact that I don't really have any idea what to do. I could try to do the same thing with my thigh that Celia just did. Would she like that? Does she want my hands?

I remember having her in my mouth under the full moon and flush just remembering it. Am I brave enough to repeat that without the influence of the moon to guide me?

I don't know if she knows that I'm paralyzed with indecision or if this is just another example of Celia knowing what she wants and taking it. "Your hand, give me your hand," she murmurs, her eyes almost feverish. Without waiting, she takes my hand in hers and positions it like she wants it, sliding two of my fingers inside her immediately, then positioning my palm so the heel of my hand presses against her clit. Her eyes flutter shut for a moment as she bites her lip, rocking her hips slightly.

I wish I knew how to talk like she does, but I have no idea what to say. My hand seems to be enough for her, and I get daring and curl the fingers inside of her. I've done it on myself before, and I can't always get the angle right, but maybe if I try really hard—

Celia groans, long and low, and I have to suppress a grin. Yes. There. That's it.

It doesn't take her long to come. She rocks on my hand, her moans getting higher and more obvious the longer things go on, and then, at last, she squeezes my fingers in the tight, warm clench of her cunt and collapses forward into me.

I raise the hand not inside of her and stroke over her short hair, trying to soothe her as she continues to make little whimpering noises.

They're adorable, really, little moans and whimpers as the aftershocks move through her body, her hips still rocking like she doesn't know if she wants more or not. When the whimpers start to sound less pleasurable, I pull my hand out, letting the river water rinse it clean.

Celia takes a moment to stand upright, then gives me a drugged smile. "Maybe that's what we both needed."

It's a piece of it, anyway, and I can feel that deep in my soul as well as my body. The intensity that she's still looking at me with lights a fire inside me, and I'm half a second from pushing my fingers back inside her to seize this moment, to cement what we've both just learned.

This is my mate, and she wants me. Needs me, maybe.

"Shore," Celia says urgently. "I need—I need to have you, and—under me—"

Whatever she wants. We walk out of the water, and I spend half a moment admiring water sluicing off her body, little droplets beading up and trailing down the skin I want to run my tongue down. Then she turns to me, the drugged look of her orgasm gone and wicked intent back on her face, and I know that, whatever happens next, the whole forest will undoubtedly hear what we get up to.

Then her steps stutter, and she stops. "What's that?"

"What's what?" She points, and I look down. "A bruise?" I ask. Surely she knows what a bruise is without having to point it out.

"Why do you have one of those?"

She sounds like it's a major catastrophe. It's already blue, which means it's about halfway through fading. It's healing just as I expected and doesn't even hurt that badly.

I shrug. "I was practicing fighting earlier. I'm not that good yet, Celia. I got knocked to the ground more than once." She watched it happen—surely she can piece it together.

"It should have faded already. Did you get harmed especially badly?" She takes a step toward me now, but all lust is gone from her eyes, replaced with a concern so sharp it feels grating.

I take a deep breath to steady myself. Now I have to come clean. "I got hurt exactly as badly as you saw. So, not that badly. But it leaves bruises."

"On children," she says slowly. "On people not fully immortal yet. But you..."

"Am fully immortal," I supply. "I don't age, I recover from injuries, and as far as I know I can't be killed in the ways a mortal can. But I just heal a little slower. Bruises last a few hours longer, for example."

"And what else?" she demands, her tone accepting no nonsense now.

"What else, what?"

"You get bruises. And what else?"

"I can break bones. I'll heal faster than a human, but I don't heal as fast as most wolves. I can suffer from the cold. It's a product of my father, I assume."

She just stares for a long moment, as if my explanation was in a foreign language. "You mean, you're basically halfway between us and a mortal?"

I shrug. "My blood would say so. I think I favor the wolf side more, though."

"You can be injured."

"So can you," I point out. "You just tend to heal faster."

"You know what I mean!" Her hand goes to her hair, tugging slightly as she half turns away from me before turning back. "Bethany, why would you keep this from me? I asked you what being half-human meant, and you didn't tell me."

"Can you blame me?"

"Yes! You know who I am. You know what's coming for us. And you're vulnerable, which makes me vulnerable."

I flinch. That sounds a little too true, but also a little too accusatory. "I'm learning to fight for a reason."

"And you're letting Callum beat the shit out of you when you know that you can be injured!"

I take a deep breath. "First of all, Callum is only working with me directly because everyone else refuses to hit me. Seems to think it would piss you off. They'll show me everything else, but they won't lay a hand on me, even if it'll help me get better. Second of all, Callum knows that this happens to me. And third, he's just as vulnerable as I am. Maybe more so. So let's not blow this out of proportion."

"Blow this out of proportion?" she asks disbelievingly, her face moving so fast I can hardly keep up with the expression. "Bethany, you're my mate and you're breakable."

She says breakable with so much venom that I physically flinch. "I'm a lot of things," I admit, mustering as much dignity as I can. "And I haven't broken yet." I turn to the mess of my clothes, sopping wet and muddy, and go to try to separate them from each other. I'm failing miserably, feeling my composure slipping through my fingers as the cloth sticks together. "I'd like to go back to the hall now."

I don't wait for her to reply. I just tug on the sopping wet clothes that stick to my skin and start walking.

CHAPTER TWENTY

CELIA

I'm left staring after her as she marches away, looking ridiculous and so determined, a combination that only makes her look more fragile.

She bruises. And she won't grow out of it someday like Callum will. I know I only have to protect him for so long. Bethany, on the other hand, will never stop being a weakness.

Does Ames already know? I suddenly regret publicly announcing her as my mate. I thought it would ensure her security in our pack, but if word gets back to Stone Village, she's just become an exploitable weakness. Ames almost certainly knew about this weakness before I did. I shouldn't have been so rash. Maybe someday it will be safe to acknowledge her publicly, but that time clearly isn't right now.

I haven't heard anything about my mate in other villages we've visited. That doesn't rule out a spy for Ames, but it does at least rule out blatant gossip as a problem. The situation is likely still salvageable. I take a few deep breaths, repeating this to myself so I can calm down.

She's gotten far away now, a speck between the trees. Her shirt was at one point yellow, and I wonder where she got it. Even covered in dirt, it still stands out.

I'm still entirely naked, but I admit I don't care half as much about that as I do about protecting Bethany. She's been out here in the woods, vulnerable and breakable, when we both know Stone Village has killers wandering around? Has Callum at least had the manners to escort her, lending her protection as they move through areas where who-knows-what could be lurking?

Pulling on clothes as I move, I follow her.

***

Dinner that night is an awkward affair. When I walk into the hall, Bethany is already cooking, seemingly having changed back into her dress and gotten right to work. To my surprise, Callum is helping her. Bryce has the foresight to ask Callum if he's heard from Heath, and when he confirms that he hasn't, I half debate just getting on my horse and leaving again. But no, I'm thinking like a spurned lover, not a queen. And I, at the very least, need to talk to Callum and ensure my mate is safe before I leave again. No one wants to broach the heavier topics, so we eat in silence until, at last, Bethany pushes away from the table.

"I have laundry to do," she says, not looking at me. "I'll bring back water for washing plates."

She turns away like we aren't even here, like she was simply speaking out loud, and goes to gather her still-sopping clothes from earlier.

"Bryce..." I mutter.

"Hm?"

"Follow her."

He drops his fork. "Are you joking?"

"No. Follow her. Be discreet, unless you want to deal with her anger."

He stares at me for a long moment, but clearly can see how serious I am by the set of my face. "Unbelievable," he mutters, but he doesn't speak out further against his queen.

Callum doesn't seem to have the same reservations. "That's bullshit, Celia," he mutters. He at least has the courtesy to keep his voice down, so when Bethany walks straight past us and out the door, she can probably hear him, but I'm certain she doesn't know what we're discussing.

"No, what's bullshit is you wielding a sword against my mate who is practically mortal."

Bryce goes very still, and I almost snap and remind him of the order I just gave him, but after a moment, he jumps to his feet and slips out the door.

Callum crosses his arms like a petulant child. "I'm practically mortal, and she wielded a sword against me. I don't see you sticking up for me."

"You could have cut her down when you were five. She's different."

"She's not even as mortal as I am," Callum says mulishly. "She bruises, Celia."

"She can break."

"Any of us can break in the right circumstances, and let's not pretend we're not living through those circumstances. So, what, she should just lie still and wait for death? Bethany's decided she's going to be prepared. I admire that." He swallows. "I like her, Celia. She's got heart."

Something in my heart squeezes at that, because it sounds uncomfortably like my little brother is trying to tell me that he knows my mate better than I do. "You have a duty to care for my mate."

"I am caring for her. I'm giving her the tools she asked for." He shrugs. "And she's returning the favor. It was about time I learned how to cook."

It's probably true, but I don't let it soften me to this. "Callum, I'm telling you to stop."

He juts his chin out, his eyes flinty. "No."

"You're saying no to me? Your queen? When you're already on thin ice for your underground paramilitary organization?"

He doesn't back down. I should have known he wouldn't; us Crae siblings are nothing if not stubborn. And now, I've threatened him with nothing to back it up. Nothing I'm willing to actually do, anyway.

"Someone has to," he says. His voice remains quiet and even, not an overt challenge, but certainly not submissive in any way. "This was supposed to be your support system, Celia. A mate and three siblings to help you. But it only works if you let us help."

"No one ever intended you to run amuck all over my decisions," I tell him. "There's one queen, Callum, and her word is final. It doesn't work if we do everything by committee."

"The queen can still hear advice, though."

"And this is you giving advice?"

"My advice for you is to figure things out with your mate. Trust her a little more. Don't send Bryce to follow her through the woods like a hunter tracking prey. And people are scared, Celia. They thought our parents would never die. We thought it. And now they have, and they don't know what's coming next."

"I can hardly divulge war plans," I say dismissively, hoping he doesn't notice me ignoring the advice about Bethany. "That is an excellent way for them to fall into enemy hands."

"First of all, start by not automatically assuming your people are spies. Second, no one is asking for battle plans, Celia. They're asking for reassurances. Trust me. I'm here with them while the rest of you aren't."

I'm not taking advice from a twenty-year-old who still sounds bitter about being left behind, who truly thinks he can never die and that he's ready to go to war, who doesn't see the danger to others. Callum is still essentially a child.

I don't have to tell him that, though, because the door opens and Bethany re-enters, a full bucket in one arm. It looks heavy. Does she experience it as heavy? Is she as strong as a normal wolf? Will that bucket actually strain her?

She sets it down and sighs. "Dishes?"

Callum stands, and doesn't take his eyes off of me as he says, "I'll take care of them, Bethany. Why don't you relax?"

She raises her eyebrow but doesn't argue. "Do we have enough wood for the night?"

"You chopped plenty. We're fine. Relax."

She nods, and it strikes me that she trusts him. She takes him at his word. Things really have changed between the two of them in just the week I've been gone, and something hot and angry coils inside me.

Jealousy, I realize after a moment. This is jealousy, and a thousand times more potent than when Bryce got praised by our father and I didn't, or when Heath got a new sword and I was stuck with my old one. This is burning like the sun, and I want to excise it from my body while knowing full well that it's not going anywhere.

Damn Callum. It's irrational, but I blame him, nonetheless.

I push to stand, looking at Bethany. "Shall we go to bed?"

I don't think I imagine the coldness in her gaze, but she doesn't air her grievances in front of the others. Or other, really, since Bryce hasn't snuck back inside yet. "Let's go."

I feel a bit like a kicked puppy when I get up to follow her to our room, and I can't say I like the feeling.

***

I lie back in bed and watch her fuss around for a moment, but at last she turns to me. "Why did Bryce follow me to the river, exactly?" she asks.

I go completely still. I should have expected that. "He needs to practice being sneaky," I mutter.

She throws up her hands. "I'm a wolf, Celia! Even if you apparently don't think so anymore. Of course I could sense someone following me, and he was practically right on my ass, not exactly being subtle. Which makes me think you don't trust me somehow. So, tell me Celia, is it because of where I'm from or what I am?"

I haven't even considered where she's from, not since she first got here. If she was a spy, she was a bad one, so I'd put that out of mind. I already know that isn't the argument to make to get back into her good graces.

"I trust you," I tell her instead, hoping that will be enough.

Instead, she laughs. "Oh, I know you don't, and that wasn't my question."

"What do you mean?" I feel control of this conversation slipping away like sand through my fingers, and no matter how hard I grasp, I can't get it back.

"Whichever reason you had your brother follow me, that is not a sign of trust." She paces a small, tight circle. This room isn't big enough, and when I look at her, all I see is a cornered wolf, and I know full well that cornered wolves are dangerous.

"You can't blame me for being worried about my mate," I say calmly, sitting up and climbing off the bed. "That's the point of a mating bond, Bethany. I'm meant to protect you."

"If you'd take anything in return, then sure! But you shut me out, Celia. You completely cut me off. You come here all cold and distant; you bring your guard down just to bring mine down before you put the walls back up again, and I'm left out in the cold. That's not a functional mating bond."

"What do you want from me?" I ask slowly, trying to pretend I'm not drowning in her words.

"I want to have a mate," she whispers. "I want this to be real, Celia. And that means trusting me. That means accepting that I'm your mate, not some new duty, even if I'm not what you thought I'd be."

That opens up something visceral and painful inside me. No wolf should ever accuse their mate of being not what they expected. We expect to have a mate, knowing our mate will be perfect for us. Fate doesn't choose wrong. We don't plan for it, and we don't make assumptions.

She looks me over coldly while I'm floundering for words. "I'm sure you'll be gone in the morning," she says, "so I'll say goodbye now."

Then, without actually saying goodbye, she leaves the room.

And just like that, I feel the last of the sand slip through my fingers.

CHAPTER TWENTY-ONE

BETHANY

I like to think I keep some dignity as I storm out of Celia's bedroom, but I doubt it.

Callum and Bryce are both sitting at the kitchen table, and it doesn't take any amount of effort to see the tension in the room. "I'm going out," I say simply. "Don't follow me again."

Bryce opens his mouth but doesn't say anything. What can he say to defend himself? That he was just following his queen's orders?

Callum is the one who speaks. "Need anything?" His voice is gentle as he says it, but not condescending. Callum's entire attitude toward me has turned around in a week, and I know that if anyone here is truly my friend, it's him.

No, Honor seems friendly, too, and Agnes has been kind to me. I might not be liked by most of the Crae siblings, but I've done all right at ingratiating myself to the pack. I'm not completely unlikable.

"I'm fine," I tell him as gently as I can, so hopefully he knows that I appreciate his support. I'm not fine, but that's irrelevant. There's nothing he can give me or do that would make this okay.

I walk out the door without another word, and it's only when I'm outside that I realize belatedly that I have nowhere to go. I could go to Honor or Agnes, but aside from being a terrible imposition, I have no desire to publicize my struggling relationship. It's embarrassing. A wolf's mating is supposed to be natural and instinctive, and I don't need one more sign that I'm a defective wolf.

And I don't need to air the Crae's dirty laundry to the pack. I have enough respect for them to keep this to myself.

Instead of trying to find a place to go, I just walk under the moonlight, letting my feet guide me to wherever they want. I won't go too far from the village center because Celia is perhaps not entirely wrong to worry about something happening. I didn't even bring a weapon, which feels like a mistake, even if I can excuse it in my hurry to get away. Right now, it hurts to admit that Celia is right about anything, but I'm not blind to the fact that we are essentially in the middle of a war right now, and we all know that Stone Village will fight dirty and wouldn't be averse to sneaking into our homes in the middle of the night.

I can't believe I said what I did. I can't believe I actually summoned the will to say the words. Not that I think she didn't deserve them—Celia certainly needed to hear it. If she'll even listen to me remains to be seen.

It's crystal clear that Celia wants a mate who requires no effort from her. She can be sweet when she's getting what she wants, when I'm a simple, easy, and quiet escape. But the minute I present as a person, the minute I add a complication, she doesn't want me anymore.

I should be satisfied with that. I should accept that having a mate means I have an indisputable place here, and leave it at that. I don't need her to love me; I just need somewhere safe.

Turns out that there's more wolf in me than anyone thought, though, because I can't quiet those mating instincts. And those instincts are screaming at me that something is wrong. They're demanding I push back and show my mate where the boundaries are so we can be a functional mated pair.

I thought mating was supposed to be easy. I thought you met, and then it was a perfect, happy life. I assumed that was the point of the wolfish instinct; it drove us to whatever would make us happy.

Maybe I'm a defective wolf. Maybe there's something wrong with me, and I'm the problem.

I wrap my arms around myself as I walk, warding off the chilly night air. Celia is probably in her bed, and I longingly think of the sweet warmth of her in bed. But no. Even if she'd let me, I'm not crawling into bed after her tonight.

I don't think I did anything wrong, is the problem. Maybe I'm not supposed to speak to the queen like that. Maybe being mated to royalty means accepting that you're always lesser than your mate.

It doesn't even matter. I'm sure she'll be gone in the morning, leaving Callum and me behind once again. I suppose that's one victory, at least; Callum seems to have whole-heartedly accepted me now.

What do I do if she's not gone in the morning? How do I go about telling her I want to mend this bridge? Or do I not say anything? Maybe I should ignore her like she ignores me.

Just the thought of it makes something painful jolt inside me. My wolfish instincts don't like that thought at all.

I keep walking, letting the moonlight guide me, but when I notice someone peering out their door when I walk by, I know I need to go back. We don't need any gossip about what does or doesn't go on in the Crae home.

So I turn back and go home, but I don't lower myself to crawling into bed with Celia. Maybe tomorrow we can start mending this bridge, but it won't be tonight.

So I sleep by the fire again, and it's a miserable night's sleep without her next to me.

CHAPTER TWENTY-TWO

CELIA

Callum and Bryce are both waiting for me at the table when I admit defeat and get out of bed, and Bethany is nowhere to be found.

It hurt badly enough to not have her in bed last night, but not seeing her out here somehow hurts worse, and I have to fight to keep walking as the pain increases.

"Where is she?"

Callum continues to eat calmly as if nothing in the world is wrong right now. "She went out."

Jealousy rears its ugly head, and only our sibling bond keeps me in check. "Did she stay with you last night?"

He actually sets his food aside for that, staring at me like I'm the dumbest person he's ever met. "No. She slept out here again. She did that when you first left her here, too, by the way. Because you never put an ounce of effort into making sure she was welcome here."

Getting scolded by Callum is the last straw. I drag my fingers through my hair, a tangled, knotted mess from all my tossing and turning last night. "I had bigger things on my mind."

Bryce, who's remained silent so far, speaks up. "I truly believe in putting the pack first," he says, "but there's nothing bigger than your mate, and you know it."

"There is when the entire pack—the entire kingdom, really—will fall apart at any moment. We have to secure this, Bryce. And I can't afford to be distracted, and I'm sorry she needs extra coddling, but I can't give it right now—"

Callum pushes his chair back and stands. "I'll talk to you next time you deign to remember us here," he says. "And by the way, short of you ordering me to stop, I'm going to keep running my army. Someone has to think about the future."

It's laughable that he really thinks he's the only one thinking about the future, that somehow his poorly trained band of wolves will really be what saves us from Ames and Stone Village. "Grow up, Callum."

"I'm working on it, if the rest of you would ever care to notice."

He doesn't give me a chance to retort; he just walks straight out. He's not dressed for the day yet, and certainly not for sword drills, but he doesn't let that stop his dramatic exit. I turn to Bryce when the door swings closed. "Do you understand what I'm saying, at least?"

He sighs, and to my horror, he pushes back from the table. "Not really. I understand you're under a lot of pressure. I understand life has not been kind to you recently and has asked so much of you. I don't understand why you're willing to risk her because of that, though."

I bite my lip. "If she was a good mate, she'd understand what I'm struggling with right now and give me grace. She'd wait for me. Aren't mates supposed to be what the other needs?"

Because Bryce can say he understands the pressure, but he doesn't. Not really. The pressure of being born first means I've protected my siblings from the reality of my situation. None of them will ever have the ultimate fate of every wolf fall on their shoulders.

No, that's just me.

"Are we staying or leaving?" he asks instead of arguing. While Bryce might not truly understand, he's at least been trying to help. And right now, he helps by keeping his mouth shut.

Everything in me pulls to go see Bethany. To ensure she's safe and okay, and to ask her what the hell she was thinking, sleeping on the floor by the fire instead of in our bed. And she and I will have this conversation. We'll work out the details, work out our differences. But not yet. She'll still be here when this is all said and done, so I have to prioritize the delicate issues in the pack first.

***

We reach yet another village around dinner, and the pack leader eagerly invites us in to eat with her.

Dinner is fish, which is common here, as this high in the mountain there are far fewer animals but plentiful fish in the river. We eat gratefully, but to my eternal disappointment, they don't even give us a moment's rest before the pack leader starts speaking.

"Stone Village is sending out runners," she says conversationally, like she's explaining who caught the fish and not an act of military aggression. "They're bringing promises."

"What are they promising you that we aren't?" Bryce asks neutrally, his pragmatism completely at odds with the bubbling fury inside me.

She shrugs. "Representation in a council, better military protection and safety, stronger trade between villages, more food access."

"None of which he'll actually give you," I bite out. Representation? Ames considers himself above everyone else. He's never going to share even a modicum of power. We only need military protection from Ames and his wolves. And as for trade, Stone Village has been known to massacre human villages when they're under-supplied for a hard winter. Isn't that how Bethany's father died? Ames isn't going to promote equitable and fair trade among all wolves. He's more likely to kill them and take what he wants.

"People believe him," she says. "It doesn't matter if it's true, Celia. It only matters what they believe."

In a way, she's right, but that doesn't change my mounting anger. "Well, then tell them not to be stupid," I snap. Bryce sucks in a sharp breath, but he doesn't interrupt me. "Tell them to use their heads. Ames and Stone Village murdered the last king and queen of the wolves, and even after doing so, couldn't seize the crown because they were too cowardly to face all of us. If Ames is willing to resort to that and can't even get what he's after, then I don't know why anyone would believe he can deliver on these ludicrous promises now."

She just blinks at me, long and slow, then tilts her head down. It's a gesture of submission, acknowledging the dangerously superior wolf, and it doesn't feel good that she feels the need to do that. But it also didn't feel good hearing her talk so casually about taking what I've worked so hard for, so I let it go.

***

"Are you absolutely insane?" Bryce hisses. "Telling them to not be so stupid?"

"I don't mean it like that... but it doesn't make it less true. If they really believe that Stone Village will help them, then—"

"Then we need to convince them we're worth something," he snaps. "They don't owe us anything unless they feel like it's deserved, Celia. You know this. You've always known this."

"You think I don't?" I'm growing less cautious about the volume of my voice, but I can't control myself entirely, not when I'm this aggravated. Byce dares to imply that I don't know the significance of my role? "You think I don't know that we are on tenuous ground and that at any second, any one of these people could topple it and that they'll get nothing in return because Stone Village won't give them a word of what they've promised? I'm fully aware of the stakes, Bryce."

"Then act like it. Ask them what they need. Listen to them talk about what life is like here, what they want, what their hopes for the future are. Listen to them, Celia, for five minutes. Before you spout off and say something stupid."

"Leave it, Bryce," I tell him, voice low, and anyone else in the world would be intelligent enough to drop the subject entirely. I never considered Bryce unintelligent, but he ignores the obvious threat and opens his mouth again, so I cut him off. "This is my duty, my destiny. I have the crown, Bryce. Therefore, I make the decision."

"You're willing to lose your crown over this?"

Bryce doesn't get it. If I don't hold the line now, if I don't keep this together, my crown will be on Ames' head, and people will be dead.

"It's my risk," I tell him, letting him know in no uncertain terms that the conversation is over.

Chapter Twenty-Three

Bethany

Celia is gone, and I'm not surprised.

To be fair, I did leave the house this morning after making absolutely no effort to see her or talk to her, so I can't say it's entirely her fault that we didn't mend bridges. And I know that's cowardly and probably counterproductive, but I admit a truly terrible night's sleep did not make me the most charitable and forgiving person.

Honor gives me a hard look when I make it to the training field. "You look like shit."

I snort. "Thank you. I always appreciate compliments."

"Sleep badly?" she asks, and it's so shrewd I tense up.

Everyone knows Celia is in town, and Honor must have witnessed the debacle that was yesterday. She saw Celia fight her brother over a bruise on me and then drag me away. And any rational wolf would assume we went home, had passionate sex, and fell asleep in each other's comforting embrace.

I think it's obvious that some of those steps got skipped.

I still don't want any rumors about us, though, so I keep my mouth pressed firmly shut. I raise an eyebrow and grab one of the practice swords, beginning to warm up by completing the footwork drills that Honor taught me.

"I wasn't sure Celia wanted you to come back," she continues.

"Being here is practical," I say, which is both true and not at all an answer to the question she's hinting at. "I'm sure Callum will be along any minute. Celia wants us to be prepared for what's coming as much as he does." Again, it's presumably the truth, although I doubt Celia and Callum see eye-to-eye on how that's done.

Thankfully, practicing the simple moves takes up a fair amount of my concentration, so Honor stops asking difficult questions.

When Callum arrives, he looks like a thundercloud is hanging over his head. He gives me a long look, raises his eyebrows, but just shrugs before turning to everyone.

"We're preparing for an attack," he says, which causes an immediate outbreak of murmurs. He holds up a hand. "Not imminent, necessarily, and I don't suddenly have any information I didn't have yesterday. But Celia is preparing for Stone Village to escalate, so we're changing our patterns. We're no longer just here to train in the abstract. Starting now, we run patrols of the village. We secure the border. We ensure that everyone is protected. And shifts start as soon as we're done establishing them, so start picking when you'd like to take your turn."

***

Callum doesn't let me patrol without him. Part of me wants to protest, but he does it without making a public scene about it, and he does it without calling out why I need a partner of his caliber.

I'm not fully trained, but I think Callum is more worried about my fragility. He's more breakable than I am, but that doesn't seem to enter his mind at all.

Guard duty is boring. Nothing happens, which I know is a positive thing, but knowing that doesn't alleviate how boring it is. Mostly, I'm just supposed to keep an open eye and not do anything else.

Callum stays close, and apparently, he wants to talk. "Did Celia throw you out of your bedroom last night?"

"I left."

"To sleep on the floor? Why would you do that? Surely you know Bryce or I would let you stay. Or Heath's room is available."

"I don't need you to save me, and I don't need to give Celia any more reason to be mad."

He purses his lips. "She's mad about the half-human thing?"

I sigh. "I don't know what she's mad about." That's the truth, too. It goes deeper than me not telling her, essentially a stranger, about my weaknesses. I think she might be mad to be stuck with a mate at all, honestly, and I'm trying not to let that tear me to pieces.

Aren't mates supposed to treasure each other?

"She'll come around," Callum says assuredly, and then he turns away from me to do a sweep of the forested land surrounding us. I assume that means our conversation is over, but Callum doesn't need to look at me to talk. "And if she doesn't, we'll kick her ass into shape."

"She's your queen, Callum."

"She was my sister first. I'm a lot younger, so I never got any of the early childhood bickering the three of them did, but that doesn't change much. If you can't be honest with your siblings, then you can't be honest with anyone."

"So, did she officially tell you that you could keep training the military? Are these patrols on her orders?" I ask, ready to change the topic from me and my struggling relationship.

"Officially? Hm, not exactly. It was more that I made a decision, and I'm sticking to it. She'd have to stay if she wants to stop me."

"You know she's leaving for official purposes, right?" I press. "She didn't abandon us, Callum."

"Didn't she?" he asks rhetorically, then sighs. "I know I'm young, Bethany. I get what everyone sees when they look at me. But even I know that our parents always intended for Celia to be queen, and us three to support her. And that means more than just saying yes. It means doing something. Bryce is supporting these meetings of hers, Heath is her spy... I just need to do something, too. It's literally my purpose."

I can't argue with that. I've seen the way he lights up doing this job, the way his mind engages. I'm worried about him, but I imagine he's worried about me in the same amount, so neither of us tries to stop the other.

Maybe that's why he insisted we be partnered together. This way, we can both look out for the other and assuage our worries.

"If I'm supposed to be a part of this family, then I need a purpose too. And as much as I've appreciated learning from you, I don't think this is it," I admit.

"Then what will it be?"

That's the unanswerable question. I have no idea.

Chapter Twenty-Four

Bethany

A week passes, then two, and I'd like to say that the distance between us grows more tolerable, but that would be a bald-faced lie.

It feels like my organs are hurting to be so far apart for so long. I want her at my side constantly, and I can't sleep without her.

Unfortunately, I can't even escape thinking about her. Every waking moment is consumed by a low, thrumming need for her, and she's always in my mind.

"Is it always like this?" I break down and complain to Agnes. I'm helping her clean out her chicken pen, and then we'll use what we find to fertilize her garden. In exchange, I'll walk away with eggs for Callum and me tonight. I honestly think it would be a good idea for us to get some of our own animals. I haven't broached it with Callum yet because that's work one of us will need to take on, and anyway I don't want Agnes to think that I don't want to help her anymore.

"Is what like what?" Agnes asks.

I flush. I shouldn't have asked because I've been working so hard to keep our business private, but now I've said it, and there's no way out. "The mating bond," I mumble. "Her being away is painful. Will it always be painful?"

She clucks her tongue. "I was wondering how you were holding up. I can't imagine being so far apart when I was newly mated. That was four or so centuries ago, of course, so I don't remember those first days perfectly, but I remember the intensity. I don't think you ever forget that."

"Early days?" I ask, brightening. "So this isn't permanent?"

"It eases," she says. "But it never goes away. It's not supposed to. You're mates, Bethany. You're supposed to be drawn to each other. Frankly, I'm surprised either of you is able to stand this arrangement."

Does Celia feel what I feel? Maybe she's just better at hiding it.

Then why won't she come home, or at the very least take me with her?

"What are you planning to do for the moon?" Agnes asks.

"The moon?" I ask, temporarily distracted, but I know quickly what she means. The moon. There's only a few days until the moon is full, and then Celia and I will be mindless under it once more.

That is, assuming she's here. What would it do to us to be so far away during the full moon? I can't see the wolf inside me being satisfied with an explanation that she has business elsewhere.

"I don't know what Celia plans," I confess. "I'm hoping she'll be home."

Agnes looks at me with what I can only describe as pity, and I bristle under the look. "For both of your sakes, I hope that's true."

***

Just when I'm debating how to restrain a wolf crazed out of their mind, Celia and Bryce ride back into the village.

They both look travel-worn and tired, but I don't think it's my imagination that Celia looks worse, like perhaps she hasn't been sleeping. It probably makes me a terrible person to be gratified by that, but I am. At least we're experiencing this situation together.

I have to fight the urge to run to her, but I have no desire to make myself look any more desperate and downtrodden than I already do. I can't quite make myself stop looking, though, which means the laundry I'm hanging to dry is abandoned entirely as they ride up to the hall.

They dismount, and one of the guards traveling with them takes the horses. I hold my breath as they approach.

"Has Heath returned?" Bryce asks me.

"Hello, Bryce. Good to see you, Bryce. I hope your journey was well. No, I haven't seen Heath here, I'm sorry to say," I tell him. Responding so sarcastically feels like a dangerous thing—I certainly never would have done it in Stone Village—but I'm supposed to be his family now. He can show me basic courtesy.

He has the good manners to look briefly abashed. "Hello, Bethany. I'm glad to see you well."

Well is an exaggeration, because even without being able to see my own face, I know the strain of the last few weeks is wearing on me.

I turn to Celia, who hasn't said a word yet and is studying me intently. "You look..." she murmurs.

I flush. "I know." She doesn't look much better.

"Would you like to go for a walk?" she asks, hesitating a moment when her eyes flick over the hall.

I swallow my pride and my anger. "I'd like that."

She nods like this is some sort of official proclamation, and then we begin to walk together. She keeps her hands loosely clasped behind her back, every inch the queen on parade. I, on the other hand, keep my hand on the pommel of the sword Callum gave me. I've been patrolling this forest for too many days now not to remain on alert.

Celia catches the gesture. "Where did you get that?"

"Callum found it for me."

"It doesn't fit you."

"I'm aware." I'm tall, but I'm thinner than most wolves I've seen. As a result, this weapon is too big and too heavy for me, but I'd accepted it gratefully. Something is better than nothing.

Celia doesn't seem to know what to do with my easy acknowledgment and dismissal. She's silent for a long moment as we continue to walk.

I want to touch her. Last time we walked together she held my arm, and it was more to drag me than anything else, but right now, I am driven to touch her with a ferocity I've never felt before. Is it the upcoming moon, the fact that I've been away from her for so long, or something else?

I force myself to resist. If she's going to leave me behind for weeks at a time, then I'm not going to be the mate who pines after her and falls into her arms at the earliest opportunity. It turns out that there's a level of pathetic that I'm not willing to reach, which is a relief to know.

"The full moon is tomorrow night," Celia eventually murmurs.

"Mhm." I don't say anymore. She's not saying anything unknown to me; every wolf knows when the moon will be full.

"I came back to spend it with you," she continues.

"You came back for information on Heath," I correct, surprising even myself with my response. The Bethany who fled Stone Village never would have thought I'd say things like that, and to the queen, of all people. But I'm not willing to grovel for safety, not here. Not in a place where fate itself says I'm supposed to be her equal.

"I'm very good at doing multiple things simultaneously. It's a job requirement," she says breezily.

Yes, perhaps it is. But if Heath had told her to meet him somewhere else, if the choice had been between me and the information she needs for her revenge? She would not have chosen me.

I can't blame her, not entirely. She's the queen, and she has loyalties she has to take care of. I cannot always be her first priority. I'd just like to be somewhere on the priority list, but unfortunately I'm very sure I'm not right now.

Still, I can make my displeasure known, but I can't do the impossible. If I turn down Celia's offer to spend the full moon together, then I'll just make a liar of myself. I won't be able to resist her, and I know it.

"We'll spend the full moon together," I concede. "Will we spend time together before then, or is your plan to ignore me until then?"

Celia flinches slightly and looks away. The cutting remark lands, and it might make me a bad person, but I'm temporarily satisfied by that reaction.

"Of course I'm going to spend time with you," she says, and my spirit is lifted by that remark, but then she continues, "Even without being here, it's obvious that you've made an impression around here. You should be at my side when I'm governing."

My heart sinks. Right. I might not be serving the powerful people here the same way I was at Stone Village, but I'm serving the needs of the powerful people just the same.

CHAPTER TWENTY-FIVE

CELIA

I think if Bethany could resist the pull to me, then she'd be avoiding me entirely. Thankfully, she's enough of a wolf that she feels the same pull I do, so she's at my side even when it's obvious she would rather be anywhere else.

She probably wants to be with Callum or Agnes. Honor seems friendly with her, too. What do they have that I don't?

They've been here, the most rational part of me knows. They've spent time with her while I've been forced to be away.

But I'm here now. And I've visited every village except Stone Village, so I'll presumably be here until I have a plan of attack. I'm eagerly waiting for Heath's return because whatever information he has is the key to both our family's revenge and the security of all wolves. But while I wait, perhaps I can get to know my mate a little better and show her that things will be better when I can be assured we're safe.

I have to believe there will come a day when the wolves are secure, and that the day will come soon. And when it comes, I dream of long mornings with Bethany in our bed. Of days bathing in the river and making her come like I did last time we were there. Of dinners with the entire family. I can take over her sword training, but it'll be unnecessary because I'll have ensured we're all safe. She won't have to worry, and I won't have to worry about her.

I can't quite let the worries go—I doubt queens ever fully do that, not in times of war—but I can use these few days to give her and me a glimpse of what the future entails.

I take her hand before we re-enter the village. She gives me a surprised look, but thankfully lets me take her hand and even gives me a small squeeze.

Bryce will lose his sanity if he hears what I intend to do today. He's made it clear that he doesn't much like how I speak with the other packs, and I know I've disappointed him in these last few weeks. I need to prove that I can still have these conversations and that I can live up to the pressure of the crown.

The people of this village like me. They always have. I grew up here, learned how to rule here, and learned everything about life here. I'm friends with these people, lifelong neighbors, and now their queen. Surely, they will react to me better than the other villages.

The other village can learn to listen to me. That's their job. But here? I need them to still like me.

Because I've seen her with my mate, and because she's been here for centuries, I start with Agnes. She's outside her home hanging laundry, and I don't hesitate to walk over. "Good morning."

She looks up. "It's afternoon."

Already we're starting on the wrong foot. I bite my tongue, not wanting this to ruin things. This needs to work.

Agnes doesn't say anything else, and I think carefully before speaking. "I've spoken to every village, and now I'm home to speak with this one. I want to hear what the needs are here."

Agnes doesn't even turn away from her laundry. "And you started with me?"

"My mate trusts you," I tell her. Bethany's hand squeezes mine, seemingly involuntarily, and I hope she knows that I mean it. That I chose my path today based on what I've seen of her.

That gets Agnes' attention. She turns to give me her attention and half a smile. "Clever," she says, an approving note in her voice. "I'm glad you see her. You're lucky she came along when she did."

I don't feel lucky. I want to; I know I should treasure my mate, that a mating bond is supposed to be the ultimate gift from fate. But the timing couldn't be worse, and I still can't forget that my mate, who is infinitely more breakable than any other wolf, is carrying a sword too big for her that she can't properly swing and thinks she's training for a war. There couldn't be worse timing, because I can't protect her and my crown simultaneously.

I don't say that, of course. Agnes has been mated for a long time now. Of course she believes that fate doesn't make mistakes.

"Franky, I'm sure Bethany's already told you what the big concern is around here."

I start at the idea that Bethany has told me anything related to the pack or that she even could. She's been here less than a month, but evidently, Agnes considers her the expert now instead of me.

"Considering the amount of work she's been doing to keep your household running," Agnes continues, absolutely blind to my reaction, "I'm sure she's told you that it's inefficient. We need a better system of trade. One person or even one family cannot do all the things needed."

"That's the biggest concern?" I blurt out. Not the wolves that stole into our village and murdered their rulers, not the wolves who threaten our entire way of life. Agnes is worried about not wanting to chop her own wood.

"Is it not a valid thought?" Agnes challenges, leaning her hand on one hip and staring me down. The stare is no different from the one she gave me and my brothers as little children running around and getting mud everywhere, and I can't say I care for the comparison. I'm not that child, and just because she's older than me doesn't mean she gets to treat me like one.

"All thoughts are valid," Bethany hurries to say, taking a step forward as if to shield me from Agnes, and I hate the idea that I need to be protected from my own subjects. "And I agree with you—there are ways we can work together more cooperatively, although we'll have to be careful—I've seen that type of situation hurt people too." Her voice is grave at the end, and I know she's thinking about Stone Village.

And somehow, that just makes me angrier. Agnes is questioning me, Bethany is protecting me, and now she's insinuating that this village could become as bad as her old home. That we could somehow fuck up on that level, like we have that type of exploitative evilness inside us.

Agnes nods before I can say something. "I don't think there's anyone more perfect to be in charge of setting it up than Bethany," she says to me. "Since she knows so much about it."

Bethany stutters, and I cut across her before she can find whatever she wants to say. "I'm in charge," I say shortly. "I handle everything to do with this pack."

Agnes doesn't look impressed. "You didn't sound interested, that's all."

"I'm interested in everything to do with the wolves and how to improve their lives."

"Celia, I can—"

"No," I cut her off. "That's my job, Bethany."

Her hand goes lax in mine. "Can I talk to you for a minute?"

I don't want to fight in front of Agnes. I don't want to fight at all—it seems like a poor use of our time—but I know she's going to do it anyway. Bethany isn't the demure and withering wolf who showed up here in the middle of my coronation, and while I respect the strength she's evidently found, it's not appropriate for us to have it out in front of others. As I learned from my parents, when you wear the crown, you have to keep these things private.

"Sure," I say, trying to sound as calm as possible. I'm doubtful that I succeed. Bethany uses our still-entwined hands to tug me away, and I follow her.

There's little privacy in a village of people with the hearing of wolves, so Bethany leads me into the woods to get away from them all. "Well?" I ask when I can no longer hear them.

"Well, what?"

She turns to look at me, and I take her in. Her eyes are burning with anger, and the set of her face, the pinch of her pale brows, makes her look like some sort of vengeful ghost. Part of me wants to step back, but I remind myself who I am and stand my ground.

"Well, what did you want to discuss, Bethany?"

I expect her to demand that I let her do whatever she and Agnes want. I expect her to demand this little bit of power. Maybe I expect her to tell me off for how I spoke out there, like Bryce has been doing for weeks now. But that's not what happens.

Instead, she asks, "Why are you so resistant to letting anyone help you?"

"Plenty of people help me. What are you on about?"

"People help you when you specifically order and control every bit of it," she contradicts. She's standing with her legs spread slightly, shoulders squared, eyes firm. A forward, aggressive fighting stance, no doubt learned from my youngest brother, who should not be teaching my mate anything of the sort. "That's not letting people help you, Celia. That's still you managing every bit of it."

She doesn't understand what she's asking me. She doesn't understand what she's entered into, which is just further proof that fate has made some sort of mistake. Not us—I could feel the pull between the two of us from across the world—but the timing. It's too early in my reign, too soon after my parents' death, too much in the middle of this war. If she doesn't understand what my role is, then she's a weakness, and I can't afford any more vulnerabilities right now.

I gesture broadly. "You heard me that day, Bethany. I took those vows. Me. It was always going to be me; it always will be me. No one took them with me, and no one can. Therefore, of course I handle it all. It all falls on me."

"Have you looked around?" she demands. "You have an entire village of people who support you. They're lining up to go to war for you. You have three siblings trying to support you. I'm trying, and I'll be the first to admit that I don't know what I'm doing, but I won't learn if you shut me out forever. Give me something, Celia."

"You can do what you want," I tell her. "Do what you have been doing. Make friends, build a life. But there's nothing you can do for me."

She steps back and gives me a look, and the fire has died out of her eyes. Now they're cold as ice as they take me in, taking my measure and certainly finding me wanting. "I hope that's not true. For your sake, for the sake of all of us, I hope that isn't true. Because that's how Ames runs his village, Celia, and how he'll run the whole kingdom if he wins it. And if you really want the wolves to stand behind you, then you need to be different from him."

"Don't compare me to that monster," I bite out, her words a stinging brand I can't shake from my skin.

"I'm the most qualified person here to make comparisons to that monster," she returns. "And I'm telling you what I see." She takes another step back. "Go talk to whoever you want however you want. Alienate every last wolf here. As you said, I'm not a part of that."

And then she leaves me there, burning with fury and pain in the middle of the woods like I'm something gross and best left forgotten.

CHAPTER TWENTY-SIX

CELIA

I should be speaking with the rest of the village about their concerns, but I can't make myself do it. Pulling together a face of competence and leadership seems beyond my reach. I'll do more damage than I already have if I try to talk to anyone.

I'm watching my entire life fall apart. My village, my crown, my mate, my destiny—and that's the rub. My life falling apart doesn't just affect me. It affects all wolves, past, current, and future.

I can't force myself to leave the woods until the sun starts to set, and I only leave then because I don't want Bryce and Callum to start looking for me. I don't want to explain anything.

I want to go home. I want to curl up in my bed, except I don't even want that, because I can't imagine my bed without Bethany in it, without her soft skin and cold feet pressed against me. And Bethany won't be coming to bed with me tonight, I already know that.

I never asked my parents how they made their mating work. To me, to all four of us kids, it just always worked. They were happy, and they were partners, and we never knew anything else. If they had a secret, if they'd worked for that, then it's too late to ask them now.

I need a secret. I need the secret to everything. How do I convince a kingdom that I see our future better than they do? That I'm the one to lead us there? How do I convince my brothers not to doubt me, and my mate to trust me, follow my lead, and wait for it to be the right time?

I go the long way around so I can approach the hall without going back through the center of the village, hoping to avoid any and all conversation. I doubt I'll be so lucky inside the house, but there's only so much a person can ask for.

I keep my head down until I'm inside, then draw up short when I see Callum and Bryce at the table. They're eating and seem to be having a civil conversation, but that's not what stops me. "Where's Bethany?"

"Isn't she with you?" Bryce asks.

I slowly shake my head. "Not for hours now." My stomach seems to drop entirely out of my body, leaving an aching, empty hole. My mate, fragile and in the middle of a war, is unaccounted for.

I see what I missed earlier. This place smells like Bethany, but it doesn't smell recent. The subtle tint of sweat, of dust from the day, the way fear and joy and boredom slightly shift a scent—none of that is present.

I take a deep draw of air, determined to find her immediately. The scent is faint, like she hasn't been anywhere near here in a while, but it's no match for my nose.

Without another word to my brothers, I turn and leave, heedless of who sees me and who's around. Let someone try to get in my way right now. With Bethany gods-know-where in gods-know-what trouble, it would take an entire army to stop me.

Anything could have happened to her. Anyone could have taken her. While she left me behind today, who's to say who caught up to her next? It could easily be someone from her old life.

I don't smell blood or pain mixed in with her scent, and that's the only thing keeping me at all rational. I can feel the wolf inside me pawing at my skin, dangerously close to the edge, and that's never a good state for any wolf to be in. If I smell a single drop of blood, I know I'll slide right over that edge.

Her scent is easy to track, and I can't scent anyone in particular around her. That doesn't mean much, of course, because whoever took her might be good at masking their scent, and even if they weren't, my ability to track my mate far outstrips tracking anyone else.

All information is telling me she left alone, but I don't let myself relax. Making assumptions like that is how Ames and his soldiers got to my parents. It's how you leave yourself vulnerable to attack, and I'm not falling for it. I won't slow down until I have her safe and back at home.

It seems like being half-human doesn't make Bethany slower than the average wolf, because it takes me all night to chase her. I know she had a substantial head start, but I am slightly impressed by how long it takes me to run her down.

The sun is breaking the horizon when I at last find her, her white-blonde hair a beacon shining through the trees. "Bethany!"

She turns to me, and a quick look confirms she's healthy and fine and also furious. "You couldn't fucking let me go?"

"Let my mate go? Never." I'd rather sit naked on a stinging anthill.

"Do you know what tonight is?" she asks, her voice getting louder. "Can you think of a single reason why I'd want to leave, Celia?"

"You're angry, I get it," I mutter. As if shouting at me in the forest and comparing me to Ames wasn't enough of a hint of how she felt, she had to go and literally run away. "This isn't how we solve problems, Bethany."

"Chasing people down and foolishly coming after them?" she challenges, arms crossing over her chest defensively.

"We both know I'll always come after you."

"Do we? I wasn't sure. I thought the odds were good you'd leave the village without even thinking about me."

I might deserve that one. I can admit I'd used my duties to evade solving our problems, but it's not like my duties aren't real. I really am the queen of the wolves. I really do need to run this kingdom, and that really means visiting the packs.

"I'll always come for you," I tell her again.

She deflates just slightly. "You couldn't have given me one more night?"

"Do you have any idea what tonight is?"

"Of course I do!" She's defensive again, and I take an instinctive step back. I shouldn't back down to anyone, but I can't help myself. I don't like that look in her eyes.

"Then you know why I won't leave you alone."

She scoffs and actually turns around to walk off again like that's somehow going to work. I take a large step and catch up to her side, grabbing her arm. She tries to jerk out of my grip, but I tighten my hold for just a second, just so she gets the message.

"You're not going off alone," I tell her, trying to channel the most calm and assured voice I can. The voice of a queen. "For one thing, it's dangerous out here."

She scoffs again. "Dangerous for someone like me, you mean."

"Dangerous for any wolf who isn't aligned with Stone Village." Maybe especially for her, but I'm not stupid enough to say it. "And for another thing, tonight is the full moon. You can't avoid it, Bethany."

She stops walking, and when I don't expect that and get thrown off balance slightly, she rips her arm out of mine. "That's exactly what I'm trying to do," she says and starts walking away again.

Chapter Twenty-Seven

Bethany

I suppose it's too much to expect that she'll let me go, and I don't make it more than a few arm's lengths before her big strides put her at my side again. I admit I'm not trying too hard to run away; it seems like a waste of energy when I know perfectly well she'll catch me.

I could scent her the entire time she was following me, and I'm not half as well trained as she is. I doubt there's anywhere I could go that she wouldn't follow.

Which means I have an uncomfortable full moon to prepare for.

The wolf will be in charge, and she won't find it uncomfortable in the slightest. If the memory of last month serves me, she'll be desperate and begging for it. Which will be all well and good in the moment, but then I'll have to live with whatever we do in the morning.

Celia doesn't even like me. How am I supposed to have sex with her again?

"Where were you going to go?" Celia asks me, following in my footsteps like we're on a stroll together.

"I didn't have a destination in mind," I say, and then, because I've already long since given up on ingratiating myself with this pack by being sweet and unassuming, I continue acerbically, "See, I've never been able to explore outside the village; I didn't get invitations to other villages. So I didn't have a good destination. That wasn't really the point."

She rolls her eyes. "What would you want with the other villages?" When I refuse to answer her, she's silent for a long moment, then says in a much softer tone, "What is the point?"

"To be away," I say, like I'm speaking to a toddler. "Tonight's the full moon, Celia, and I have no desire to spend it together."

"And you think your wolf will let you spend the full moon away from your mate? Sweetheart, my instincts would make me hunt you down across the entire continent if we were separated. There is no such thing as not being together."

"Well, at least your wolf wants me around, then," I say quietly. I mean it to be cutting, but I know it comes across as pathetic, and I hate myself for it.

"What does that mean?"

"You don't want me. I'm an inconvenience to you, and you won't let me in, wouldn't treat me like an actual mate if your life depended on it. But at least you'll fuck me when you're all but mindless under the full moon."

The air is heavy between us for a long, long moment, but I refuse to stop walking. Celia hasn't tried to steer me back toward her village, but I don't see any point in going somewhere else if she's just going to follow me, regardless. Even so, I don't turn around; at this point, it's the principle of the matter.

I don't have anywhere to go. No one is waiting to welcome me into their home. No one is expecting me around their table. There is nowhere safe for me, and I'm left adrift like I was before I found Celia and her pack.

Can I count them as mine? Agnes thinks I can. Callum thinks I can, and so does Honor and all the rest of Callum's soldiers. I think even Bryce does, despite not saying anything and following me to the river that night. I certainly set out to do what I wanted to when I fled Stone Village; there is a place that will take me in. There is a place that will trade my labor for safety. I have a place for my mother when she's ready to join me.

And now I somehow want more than that. I'm getting greedy.

The wolfish instincts inside me are already pushing for me to rub against my mate, the looming full moon apparently making me feral even with hours and hours to go.

Does Celia even feel the same? She's hiding it well if she does.

Then again, she tracked me this far.

"I do want you," she says quietly. "I just can't prioritize what I want over my crown, Bethany."

"I'm not asking you to betray your crown! I'd serve the crown at your side. That's what mates do, if I understand correctly."

She exhales deeply. "None of you get it."

The patronizing tone rankles me, but at least she's not just saying that I don't get it. She's counting me among her brothers and probably the rest of the village, so I choose not to take offense. "Explain it to me then."

"The crown is the most important thing I'll ever do," she says lowly, and my step stutters when I realize that she's actually explaining like I asked. I hasten, not wanting to make her stop. I keep walking and don't look at her, letting her have her space to say what she needs. "It consumes everything about me. I knew it would. I knew what the cost would be. And I can't focus on anything else, not if it takes away from being the queen. And that includes my mate."

"We're supposed to make you stronger," I say as gently as I can. I might not have been raised alongside Celia and her brothers, and I might not know about royalty, but I do know this much. "We're not supposed to take something away or be a burden, Celia. We're supposed to help."

"No one can help with this. There's only me. That's the point, Bethany. One of us had to take this on, and it's me. I was born first, so it's my responsibility, and I have to look out for the best interest of the wolves." She darts a quick glance at me, there and away, and I pretend not to notice. "It's not that I don't want a mate. No one passes up what fate gives them; we all know you and I are meant for each other. But the timing—I have to prioritize the wolves. And that means locking in the commitment of the villages. That means handling Stone Village and avenging my parents. And that means convincing the wolves to trust my rule. I can't be selfish now."

I take a deep breath so I don't say something too rash. "Your definition of selfish needs some work," I tell her. "I think it's more selfish to hear you could have help and not take it because you're so convinced only you can do this."

"You're not listening. I am the only one who can do it. The responsibility fell on me."

"Did your father reign alone?" I interrupt the tired argument. No doubt it sounds convincing in her mind, but I'm done hearing it.

"No," she says slowly, clearly wondering what direction I've taken our conversation.

"Your parents were a pair. They were mates, and they ruled like it," I press. I hope this is true; I certainly never witnessed it. But from what I've heard around the village, it sounds to be true.

"They had a more stable situation. They had the time and energy to commit to such things."

"Callum wants to lead your army. Bryce wants to help you sort out the other villages. Heath is already helping. And I... well, I don't know what I'm good at yet," I admit, because I don't want to lie to her. "But I'll find out. As a start, I want to help you. Be at your side and help, not be left behind and forgotten except when you're feeling lonely."

"Callum is going to get himself killed, and Bryce can't work without my authority backing him. Heath is... well, okay, Heath is probably doing great as a spy. He's always been good at that. But I still need to make those decisions."

"Callum needs more time," I admit, because his youth worries me too, "But writing him off is a mistake. Give Bryce the authority to do what's needed. Unless you don't trust him. But from what I see, he's your greatest supporter."

"Not you?"

"What?"

"Aren't you supposed to say that you are my biggest supporter?"

"I'm not trying to manipulate you, Celia. I've known you for a month, and I already admitted that I don't know how to help." I turn fully to her now because I need her to hear this part. Or I need to say it; I'm not sure which. She does me the courtesy of stopping so she can look back at me. "Fate says we're perfect for each other. That we're made for each other. I shouldn't have to manipulate you into thinking that I'm here to support you; you should already know it. I might not be the most experienced in how a proper relationship works between wolves, but you and I both know that your mate is supposed to be the one person you can trust, no matter what happens."

"I do trust you."

"Don't lie to me," I tell her, but the fight is burned out of me. I can't even muster the proper energy to be angry when saying it. I'm just tired now. "I'm an inconvenience to you, not an asset. If I was, you would have let me in even once. And you wouldn't have had Bryce follow me that night."

"Forgive me, I was worried my mate, who is more breakable than most wolves, would be hurt in the war we're in the middle of. Did you forget that, Bethany? That people snuck into the village and murdered my parents to destabilize the crown? And you told us from the start that Ames would have no concerns about murdering you. Forgive me for being worried."

"Ames isn't going to seek me out to murder me. I'm not important to him."

"He would to get to me. Don't you get it? This is what I mean. The crown is heavy and has a cost, and that cost is my sanity. I want you, Bethany. But I can't ignore that you're..." She doesn't finish the sentence.

I finish it for her, her words ringing out clear as day even if she won't say them. "A weakness," I finish for her, words dull even if I refuse to let my eyes fall.

The words hurt, and I can't deny that. Fate paired me with Celia. We're supposed to be perfect for each other. But this is what she's been thinking the whole time. She's been calling me a weakness in her mind. And not just to her; to all the wolves. To the continuation of the crown.

She doesn't deny it, and I don't know if it's better or worse than her trying to make up some excuse. "I bruise," I tell her. "I get cold. I'm perhaps not always as strong as some other wolves, but I'm not weak. And I know people, Celia. I know what Agnes was talking about yesterday. If you listened, I could help you. If you talked to me, I'd know you, and I could help you more." I'm silent for a second, then press, "Your parents didn't rule alone. Why should you have to?"

"My parents," she says slowly, like she's dragging the words out of herself. It takes her a second to keep going, as if even talking about them is too much. "My parents didn't rule alone, and that didn't save them."

The air is heavy between us, and her eyes go distant. I know she's back to that terrible day.

"It didn't kill them either, Celia," I murmur. I don't know if it's the right thing to say or even if it's any of my business to say it. Perhaps I really should leave well enough alone and accept that it's not my place. Or maybe she needs to hear it.

"You don't even know how they died," she snaps. "You weren't there."

She's not truly angry at me, I have to remind myself. Not for this, at least. She's not blaming me for not being there; she's just angry.

"How did they die?" I ask, because I feel like she's daring me to. Maybe she needs to say it.

"Ames or one of his men lit a fire," she says, voice dull now, almost distant, like the memory is consuming her. "Not anyone's house, but close enough. My parents saw it first, and they ran out there. We followed them. They were unarmed, and then..." Her voice trails off, and I don't need her to finish the thought.

Ames and his men slayed her parents in front of her.

"They left," she says dully. "Ran like cowards while we were preoccupied. Ames was too much of a coward to issue a proper challenge. My parents ruled together, and they fought together, and they died together. It wasn't enough."

"I'm sorry," I whisper. There's nothing else to say.

I could say that dying together is probably how they wanted to go. I could say that ruling together probably made their life worthwhile. I could try to get Celia to see sense, but right now, when it's clear that all she can see is her parents' bodies, that seems like a cruel waste of both of our times.

She's silent as we keep walking. She keeps pace with me, even though I doubt either of us has a single idea of where we're going. The sun is high overhead before she speaks. "This has all been so sudden," she admits. "I didn't expect to rule for... truly I think part of me still thought it'd never happen. Centuries more, at least. And to find us plunging to war, and Callum going through whatever this is, and then finding you—that's a lot, sweetheart."

"Then let us help you," I tell her. "Give us some of the burden. That's the point, Celia. That's why you have people around you."

Even I, the least prepared and least qualified of the four people in Celia's household, know what I want to tell her. To relax. To listen to people when they talk to her. To not treat every wolf as an adversary to be conquered. To trust us.

I can help Agnes with her idea about trade, at least within our village. Maybe if that works, we can turn to Bryce about expanding it. Bryce, meanwhile, can go undo whatever damage has been done to the other villages and try to convince them that Celia is a better option than Stone Village. Callum can keep training his army, although I do agree with Celia that I'm worried about him marching off to war. Maybe Heath could work with him when he returns.

She's quiet for a long moment, and we keep walking onward. I don't talk, letting her think. Even in the little time we've had together, I know she needs time and quiet to think things through.

"When we get back, we should sit down, the five of us. Make a plan."

It's not much, and yet it feels like a huge win. It feels like the sun itself, honestly. "All right. I'd be happy to."

"Agnes wants you to organize trade within the village."

I shrug. "I think she just sees what I've been doing. It's a lot of work to keep a home running, Celia. And Callum has been helping now, but he wasn't at first."

"That little shit," she mutters.

I debate letting it go, but that seems counterproductive. "I didn't see any of the rest of you helping either."

"Fair point," she admits after a moment. "So, tell me what you're thinking."

"There's value in everyone having their place," I say slowly. "That everyone has a piece of the larger whole. Someone raises chickens and someone else grows grain. A group handles laundry, someone chops wood. It's one thing if a family breaks the chores up among themselves, but wolves just don't usually have that many children."

"True. Us being triplets was somewhat unexpected," she says dryly. "So, a trade system?"

"It makes sense, doesn't it?" I say. "Actual wolves are cooperative. We should be, too. The only issue is ensuring it's truly fair. Stone Village is cooperative, but only in that people Ames doesn't respect give up their labor for nothing in return."

"You think I could run a village like Ames." Her voice sounds almost neutral. It sounds almost like she's just asking. It's the calmest I've heard her while discussing Ames.

I give her the courtesy of being calm back, which means thinking before I speak. "I think Ames runs his village the way he does deliberately. But I think it's a mistake to believe you can't get similar results without trying to. I think goodness takes hard work, Celia. Unfortunately, it doesn't seem like goodness comes without that work, which means if we don't protect it deliberately, then we lose it."

She walks silently for a minute, and I study her for signs I've upset her. It always seems that way, that we get to a certain point in the conversation where she gets upset, but it doesn't seem to be coming today. Maybe we really have struck a new chord. "That's cynical, Bethany." It doesn't sound like a criticism, though.

I shrug. "I've seen what I've seen. I'm thirty-five. I know I'm not old. But my life has been brutal. I don't remember my father's village being murdered, but it happened. I worked day in and day out for Stone Village. My mother sacrificed so much to keep us both safe, and she wouldn't even run with me, determined to protect me by staying."

"And we didn't help," she says, surprising me when she says what I wasn't willing to. While I gape at her, she shrugs. "Let's not pretend. I know you haven't felt welcomed. You just said that none of us helped you, and you did all the work of keeping the household running. I get your point, sweetheart. We didn't intend badly, but we didn't do good, either."

146

Something inside me eases when she says it all without any prompting or explanation from me. She gets it. She understands. "We have time to do better."

I come to a complete stop when she reaches across the small gap between the two of us and grasps my hand. "All the time in the world," she agrees, squeezing my hand. I squeeze back, marveling at the feel of the warm, calloused skin against mine. Calluses must be formed before one reaches their immortality. Are these from a sword? Swinging an ax? I spend a moment imagining the early days of my mate.

"You really just wanted to get away from me tonight?" Celia asks softly.

"I don't know anywhere else to go," I remind her, evading the question.

"So, you truly just wanted to be away from me."

"I didn't want to... do that... with someone I felt didn't like me very much."

"And now?"

Now? Now, I think there might be promise here. We're not perfect, but perfect seems like a lofty goal and not one I could rightly expect so soon. But we are something, and it's something that I think is worthwhile.

"Should we turn around?" I ask instead of explaining.

Celia looks up at the sky through the tree canopy. "We can," she agrees. "But I don't think it's going to make that much of a difference."

"Why not?"

"Because moonrise is soon," she says. "And there's no way we can make it back first."

CHAPTER TWENTY-EIGHT

CELIA

She looks alarmed at my pronouncement, but I feel nothing but a soft peace.

Maybe this is what we need. Maybe I've been too invested in the rational part of my mind—the part of me that needs to be a queen—and I've let everything else slip. Maybe I need to let my instinct run free for a night.

Maybe Bethany is right. Maybe what I really need is her.

Being out here is hardly a problem. We'd have spent tonight under the trees regardless of whether we were here or around the village. I suppose we're more vulnerable out here, but any wolf is a fool to cross me with my instincts that close to the surface and my mate right there. I'll tear them apart with my teeth and think nothing of it in that state.

We've been stumbling around out here all day, hardly paying attention to anything, and no one's attacked us. I doubt tonight will be a problem.

Unless, of course, Bethany isn't alarmed at being out this far from home, but rather is alarmed by being out here with me.

I can't even say I blame her for wanting to leave me. We've failed her, again and again. I've failed her, and while I have a thousand excuses, I know in my heart of hearts that my parents would never have forgiven me for failing my mate.

I was raised to put my duty first, but perhaps Bethany is right. Perhaps I don't have to do it alone.

Tonight, I need to take care of my mate. I need to show her that being out here with me isn't a tragedy.

A full moon should be fun. We should be teasing each other, riling each other up. If she runs away, it should be because she knows I'll chase, and she wants that. We should be desperate for each other in every sense of the word.

Instead, I have a mate who's holding my hand tight enough that my bones creak slightly, and I don't think it's excitement leading to that.

I have a sinking suspicion I can guess why. And it's not just because she's not sure if I'm worth liking. "Sweetheart, tell me the truth. Was last full moon your first time?"

She squeezes my hand again. "Yes," she says shortly. "And thank the gods for that."

That's a response I didn't expect, considering I was beginning to believe she hadn't enjoyed our time together. "Why thank the gods?"

"Because Stone Village has a pecking order. And if you're at the bottom, and someone takes an interest in you... it can be very hard to say no."

I swallow the bile rising in my throat. "You've seen that happen?"

"Yes. And it didn't happen to me, and I'm grateful."

And now I look like a good option in comparison, which doesn't help my nausea. I don't want to be good by comparison. I want to actually be good. I want to make her heart flutter and her pulse race. I want to make her smile. I want to...

I want to complete her and let her complete me. And that means sharing burdens with her like she wants, and it means sharing our bed at night, and it means sharing something fun under the full moon.

It doesn't mean being the best option on a list of bad options.

"Do you want me to leave?" I ask her. "I can try to leave you alone for the full moon. We don't have a lot of time, but if we run in opposite directions..."

"No," she says, so decisive and clear. "No, I don't want that. I want this. I'm inexperienced but not helpless, Celia. I've made up my mind."

And she's made it up on me. It still feels uncomfortably too close to choosing the best of bad options, but at least she's choosing.

I'll convince her I'm a worthy choice. It won't be quick, but that's the point. It should take a while. I'll go slow, be steady, and show her that this is real. We'll build the type of world we want to actually live in, and then we'll live in it for a long, long time.

My mind goes soft at that thought, and it takes me an embarrassingly long time to realize I'm not just sinking into the daydream. I'm already starting to lose my grip on my mind, the wolfish, more animal instincts pushing me away.

A quick glance up confirms it. I can't see the moon through the trees, but the faint silvery light on the horizon tells me that the moon has risen.

I'm glad she chose to stay, because there's no possible way we could separate far enough for our wolf instincts to not compel us back together now.

"Are you ready for this?" I ask her. Even my voice sounds foggy, distant, and separated from me, like my mind doesn't perceive my voice—a very human part of me—as real anymore.

Bethany turns to look at me, and I can see in her eyes that the moon has her in its grip. Her light eyes are blown wide, more pupil than blue, and there's a hunger in them I've never seen before.

The wolf inside me preens. After all, it's me she's hungry for, and I'm ready to be her whole damn meal.

Just before I can figure out what our next steps should be, Bethany pushes forward and tumbles us both to the ground with one strong shove.

I yelp at the unexpected force, then wrap her in my arms so I land on my back with her on top of me. She lands straddling me, blinking in confusion before rutting her hips lightly.

She's still dressed, and so am I, so I work my fingers into her trousers, delighted to find her wet and hot and waiting for me. She moans, tilting her hips to search out my fingers, but I withdraw them and suck them into my mouth, desperate for a taste of her.

I've been a fool not to do this every day. What could be a bigger priority than tasting her, then letting her know she's mine?

There's something in my mind that tells me I have a reason, but I can't think of it right now. I don't want to think about it. I just want to be here with her.

And without all these damned clothes in the way. Why are we still dressed? Why did we even get dressed in the first place?

I shove my hand under her clothes. I need them gone. I yank at the fabric, then run my fingers up the naked skin underneath. She shivers under my touch, delicate and gasping, and I grin triumphantly at her.

She smiles shakily back at me. My mind has gone soft, not able to remember any details but the here and now, but there's one crucial piece that remains: last month was Bethany's first time. She's only had sex twice, both times with me. I need to make this good for her, make it something she wants.

A shaky smile just won't do. I need to make her wild, need to make her moan and scream so loud the animals flee the forest around us. I need to make this matter to her.

I push her blouse up to her breasts, and she pushes it the rest of the way off. It ends up discarded on the ground somewhere, but I have no idea where because my mind is entirely occupied with the sight before me.

Bethany is thin, without much meat on her bones, and she has small breasts that perfectly fit her frame. I rock my hips, moving her body just to watch her breasts bounce the slightest bit, eyes rapt. I want them in my hands. I want them in my mouth. I sit up, my movement sudden enough that it startles Bethany, but my hands go to her hips to steady her until I have her seated on my lap. Then I palm her breasts, first one, then the other, then run careful fingers over them until I hear her moan.

That's it, pretty girl. I have you. I can't actually make the words come, not like this, but I hope she knows then, anyway.

She starts to grab at my shirt, wanting it gone. I refuse to surrender my task until she bats my hands away, growling low at me.

It's not a threat, not really, but it does something to the wolf inside me, regardless. I want to roll over and show my mate my belly. I want to present my neck to her.

Would she bite me? Would I want that? I hazily recall avoiding it the last full moon, but maybe this one is different.

She doesn't demand my throat, contenting herself with stripping me of my clothes. She moves from my lap, and I growl right back, but she evidently doesn't respond to my growl in the same way I do to hers because all she does is smile and take off the rest of her clothes.

I still have trousers on, so I lay back and arch my hips, working them off. I go slow, but only because I'm watching her the entire time. She seems to know, watching me with a teasing smile as she takes her trousers off slowly, exposing her milky skin inch by inch.

At last, she's naked, glorious and beautiful. She's the moon come to life, all pale skin and pale hair and a perfect body I want to worship. I scramble to finally free myself from my clothes, desperate and hungry for her in a way I've never been before.

Before I even finish kicking them off my feet, Bethany is straddling me, that wicked smile still on her face. I let her pin me down, intent on seeing what she's going to do next, even as my wolfish instincts are nipping at me to pin her down and taste her. Soon, but she can have her moment to explore first. She can be in charge for the moment. I'll give her whatever she wants.

Her fingers trace a line of fire from my collarbone to my navel, then back up, stopping to tease over my breasts. She runs the very tip of her finger over my left nipple, causing me to growl at her again. She just smiles, then rocks her hips against mine like a reward.

She must like it, because her eyelids flutter closed, her delicate, nearly invisible eyelashes brushing the tops of her cheeks. I reach for her hip so I can guide her to keep moving. She's not giving me anything to rub against, but that hardly matters right now. I just want her to come; I'm practically salivating for it.

Then she grinds against me once more, and there's no *practically* about it. She's wet enough that I can feel it on my skin, smell her on my body, and I'm feral for her, desperate.

Her eyes widen with shock when I flip her onto her back. Before she can muster up the energy for words or even another growl, I straddle her left thigh, gently coaxing her right one up and resting it on my shoulder. Her calves are soft as butterfly wings, and I take a second to stroke over her skin before I show her why I've put us in this position.

She groans, her head falling back and eyes closing in bliss when I rock our cunts together. I can't hide my smirk, the hand not holding her calf sliding up her stomach in a slow tease. I want to touch every inch of her, taste every piece. I want to consume her and be consumed.

I keep grinding against her, chasing the look in her eyes. I need her to come, to fall apart for me. I need to hear her, to feel her, to live in a world where I provide that to her, only I provide that—

Her desperate and surprised mewl is as sweet as her growl, and I keep grinding against her as she comes. I'm close, I'm so close, just a little more, and—

I hold her leg for dear life while I ride out my orgasm, needing something to ground me as my body shakes apart.

Her hand reaches for my face, her fingers a gentle caress against my skin, and I shakily turn to try to get them in my mouth. Her fingers ghost over my lips, and her leg slides down from my shoulder, landing around my waist.

And then she uses that leg to flip me, moving so fast I don't see it coming, and I'm left stunned, looking up at her grinning face.

She moves down my body slowly, her lips pausing at my neck, my breasts, my navel, and each hip bone before she finally settles between my thighs, eating my wet cunt like she's starving.

I groan, arching up against her. My mind is already going hazy and soft again, and all I can think is the pleasure and that I want my turn, that I'm desperate to taste her, then *yes, yes, yes*—

CHAPTER TWENTY-NINE

BETHANY

I wake up drowning in the taste of her, the moon slipping below the horizon and releasing us from its iron grip.

We're so far from home, and the forest is as silent as a grave around us. We must have been loud enough to scare off any living creature within shouting distance.

I'm naked in the dirt, but Celia has once again kept me plenty warm. She's draped across me like the most luxurious blanket, and I sink further into her warmth even as I know we need to move.

I can't kidnap the queen. Celia is needed back home, and I have no desire for the other Crae siblings to hunt me down. I should wake her up so we can go home.

I can't quite make myself do it, though. If she's anything like me, she's slept poorly these last few weeks, and she's so peaceful right now. The little soft inhalations tickling across my skin tell me she's deep in her dreams.

Does she dream of us? Is she dreaming about last night, or something that hasn't happened yet?

I close my eyes and let her weight push me down. That sounds nice. I can see us waking up like this in the future, only we're in an actual bed instead of the forest floor, and the world is putting a little less pressure on her shoulders. Things will get better. We'll sleep more. Our bed will always be warm, her skin will always be soft, her hands ever so slightly rough.

It's a good dream, and I let myself sink into it. I don't sleep, but I float there in the dream until Celia at last stirs.

She presses kisses to my neck, her nose moving my hair aside so she can reach my skin. Her little breaths tickle my skin, but I can't help but realize that there's no bite there. Now that she's drawing attention right to where a bite should have gone, I can't stop thinking about it.

That's two full moons without her marking me as her mate. I want to turn and check her neck, but I already know I won't see a mark there from me, either. The moon makes us feral, but it doesn't make us forget. I know full well that neither of us bit the other.

A wolf bites another wolf as a sign of possession, a frenzied rush of mine. The marks heal over fast, of course, but leaving a lasting mark isn't what matters. It's not about what others can see. We'd know. We'd know we felt that way, and our bond would be unbreakable.

I forcibly put it out of my mind, which is made easier as she continues to kiss my skin, then finding my earlobe and sucking lightly at the skin, nipping it gently before releasing.

"We need to get you back," I murmur, loathe to break the silence but knowing it needs to be done. "I'm sure people are looking for you."

She groans, which sends pleasant vibrations through my skin. "This is the first time I've felt peace since... well, you know. And you want to take it away again?"

Her words make my heart soften. "I know," I commiserate. I don't, not really, but I can empathize with sleeping well for the first time in too long. "But things will be better. I'll help you."

I hold my breath for a moment. It's exactly what we discussed yesterday before moonrise; now I have to see if it means anything, or if words are cheap. But she sighs and sits up, leaving me bereft and cold when released from her comforting weight.

I look down at myself for the first time and see the layer of dirt covering most of my skin. I frown. "Can we bathe before we go, you think?"

"I think Bryce would be insulted if we went home smelling like this." My stomach takes that moment to growl, and she smiles. "And I can find us something. Do you get hungrier faster than most wolves?"

I shrug, because I don't want to explain that I've probably gone without eating far more frequently in my life than she has. Instead, I extend a hand, letting her help me up, and we set off looking for a place to bathe.

***

Clean, fed, and dressed in still-dirty clothes, we walk back to the village. Celia unerringly turns toward it without a second's hesitation. When she catches me watching in befuddlement, she chuckles. "I could find home from anywhere, I think," she confirms. "It's baked into my bones. Travelers use the stars to guide them home, but I just know where it is. I don't think I could ever truly leave."

"That's amazing," I whisper, thinking of what that means. Home is such a nebulous, loose concept to me. Stone Village was where I lived, and I had my mother tying me there, but it wasn't home.

I would love to always know how to find my way home. Right now, I can only guess where my mother is in the world.

Celia doesn't understand my amazement and just shrugs. "It's my kingdom. Part of the reason I've always known that I'm meant to do this. But it'll take us the better part of the day to walk there."

I look around. "We walked a full day to get here."

She gives me a mischievous smile, one I've never seen from her before. I decide I like it, even if it's gone quickly. "You walked in circles a bit, sweetheart. You weren't exactly in a straight line."

Well, fuck. I can't even run away correctly.

Celia nudges my shoulder. "I'm going to assume you subconsciously didn't want to leave."

Well, that much is true, and it's not that subconscious. I knew the moment I walked out that I didn't want to, even as I strongly felt I needed to.

Hesitantly, I reach for her hand, unsure if the easy camaraderie of yesterday will survive into the light of today.

Her grip is warm and sure, and we walk in silence for a while. I can't stop worrying about what she's thinking. Is she thinking about last night? Or maybe she's thinking about the things we talked about before that? Or maybe she's not thinking about anything related to me at all, and I'm just self-centered.

At last, I can't help but ask her. I need to know where we stand. "When we get home, what's next?" I ask quietly.

She squeezes my hand. "I think we're both entitled to some sleep and a good meal, if my brothers managed to put together some food. And then we can sit down together, the four of us. We can make a plan."

"What kind of plan?" I ask, and I wait for her to tell me that we'll discuss it later. I'm well aware that Bryce and even Callum are more valuable as a co-planner than I am and that, as good as last night was, I'm still the unexpected accessory that Celia doesn't know what to do with. But, to my surprise, she doesn't brush me aside.

"I have to find a way to deal with Callum's army," she says slowly, and it doesn't sound like she's telling me what will happen so much as inviting me in to think about it with her.

"Does it need to change?" I ask her, hoping I really am invited to contribute.

"He could die, Bethany."

"Anyone can die."

"You know what I mean."

I do. Callum is too young for what he's doing, and I know it. "Maybe one of you could be in charge? Just for now, at least. Until he's ready for it back. But I don't think his ideas are wrong."

"No," she admits, "I don't think he's wrong either. Ames is obviously a threat, but maybe he's not wrong that there will always be threats from where we least expect them." She doesn't need to repeat her story from yesterday for me to understand.

I don't know if an army could have saved her parents. Maybe Ames' sneaky, cruel, cowardly ways would have always won that day. But perhaps people will feel safer with an army present.

"And the rest of it?" I ask.

"Bryce and I need to make a plan to revisit the villages. You're not wrong, sweetheart," she admits. "I've been too focused on the war when that's not what they need. They need someone who can rule after the war. Who can be a better option than Ames."

"Mhm."

"Which is why I think I should start with our village. With you."

"Me?"

She nods. "And Agnes. And whoever else you think I should talk to. The best place to start is probably with the people who know me best. If I can't give them what they need, then I really have no hope of doing it anywhere else."

I doubt she notices, but her hand tightens on mine when she says that, panic evidence in her steps. I rub my thumb along her knuckles, trying to soothe her. I know now what I should have seen before; Celia has no idea if she can do this. She is consumed with doubt, and I am meant to be her voice of reason.

I can do that by telling her when she makes a mistake, but I can also do it by supporting her when she needs it. "You'll be great," I say quietly. "You are exactly the queen they need."

Her step stutters, and her hand goes completely lax in mine. "Gods, I hope so," she whispers, voice choked up.

I let the two of us just stand there for a moment, letting her really hear what I said. Then I squeeze her hand again. "Let's go make it happen."

***

It's well past sundown when we stumble back into the village. Celia looks like she just woke up from a restful sleep, but I'm worn out and exhausted. At least I know I can sleep tonight. With Celia by my side, I'll sleep well.

The village is unexpectedly quiet. Most people seem to be in their homes for the night, and the village center is eerily quiet. Then I remember it's the day after the full moon, and of course, mated wolves aren't out and about. They're resting, like we should be.

Unfortunately, that seems impossible, because when Celia pushes open the door to the hall, all three brothers are sitting around the table.

Callum, Bryce, and Heath. The last brother I barely know at all, but he's identical to Bryce, just with longer hair. And right now, he certainly looks as serious as his brother always does.

"Where've you been?" he asks, not giving us even a second to finish closing the door behind us.

"Full moon," Celia says shortly. "Status report?" She still has my hand in hers, and she steers me toward the table, guiding the two of us into two of the remaining chairs. She drops my hand once we're seated, folding her own hands together on the table. I'm left bereft. I don't blame her, of course, because she's been waiting for Heath's return and the information he's bringing, but I've had her hand in mine all day, and it feels like I'm naked now without it.

"I found my way in," Heath says, getting right to business. "Took a while." He turns to me. "The tip about the river was helpful, thanks."

I shiver at just the thought. Yes, I'm the one who told them about the weakness in the wall by the river, but I can't imagine him using it. It worked for me because I'd used it a hundred times before. How on earth does someone like Heath—big, powerful, noticeable, and undeniably not belonging there—use it and successfully enter the village without getting caught?

"A while," Celia repeats sharply. "It's been a month, Heath."

"Good things take time. I had to learn my way around, get information without getting caught." He sounds so calm as he says it, but I can't imagine it was anything less than utterly nerve-racking.

"And what did you learn?"

Bryce and Callum just watch the back-and-forth, and I wonder if they already know what Heath is about to say. How long ago did he get here? Did my attempt to run away delay Celia from getting the news she's been waiting so anxiously for?

Bizarrely, Heath turns to me instead of answering his sister. "Your mother is all right."

My breath catches. "You saw her?"

"Saw her? I spoke with her. A lot, actually. Bernice was my source. Couldn't have found a better one."

No, I suppose he couldn't have. My mother might not be part of Ames' inner circle or be able to make any decisions, but she does hear more than almost anyone else. Ames has never quite been aware of how much he inadvertently tells her.

"That was reckless," I manage to scold, but it sounds hollow and I'm sure everyone knows it. Knowing he talked to my mother, having any sort of news about her at all—it means so much to me, likely more than they could ever know.

Then again, everyone in this room recently lost their mother. Maybe they do understand.

"What did she tell you?" Celia asks, bringing us back to the business at hand.

"Ames is being close-lipped, but there's talk of him and some of the closest to him leaving soon. Presumably, they'll march here—he can't go any further in his quest if he doesn't take you out, Celia. I was thinking it would be a face-to-face challenge, but Bernice isn't convinced Ames is honorable enough for that. If he didn't challenge Mom and Dad, she's not convinced he'll bother to challenge you, either. Which means we need to be prepared for a sneak-attack."

"I have guards set," Callum says smoothly, and Heath raises an eyebrow. I brace myself for him to start an argument with Callum the way Celia and Bryce have, but it doesn't come. "But we're not waiting for them to come here, are we?"

"No," Celia says in a voice that books no argument. "What's the best plan of attack, Heath?"

He shrugs. "I can get three or four people through the gap in the wall with me. Bernice agreed to a signal of a white cloth tied in the tree that overhangs the river; once she sees it, she says she can distract Ames while I and a few others sneak our way in. After that, we can throw the front gate open, and you and an army can march right in and challenge Ames. It's not elegant, but it'll work."

"We can make that happen," Bryce agrees. "Celia, are you prepared to take him one on one?"

She squares her shoulders. "Of course I am."

My heart climbs up into my throat. "Is that necessary?"

"Of course it is. Challenges are settled in single combat. They always have been," she says, like she thinks my mind is addled.

"Yes, but you're the queen. Surely, you don't have anything to prove like a challenger does. You'll have an army behind you; why risk yourself?"

Her lips thin and her spine straightens, like an invisible hand is pressing against her back. "I can take care of myself, Bethany."

I know she can fight. I saw her with Callum, and I know she was holding back that day even as her skill took my breath away. I know she was raised for this, and I know she knows what she's doing. But that doesn't change the fact that Ames is a threat. Ames killed their parents, who surely were just as prepared and had more life experience to boot.

Bryce clears his throat, ever the peace-maker ready to head off an argument between us. "There will always be questions of whether Celia deserves her crown if she can't take him on in single combat," he says. "Besides, she will have an army behind her, but it's not much of one. If she can quell Ames—when she quells Ames—the rest of his people will likely fall in line, limiting bloodshed on both sides. We need that."

"Plus," Callum says, "Ames has been avoiding single combat. He's a coward. My guess is he's not as strong as he wants people to believe. If Celia's ready to fight him, she already has the advantage."

"Don't underestimate him," I say. I'm grateful that they're genuinely taking the time to reassure me instead of dismissing my concerns, but if their plan hinges on Ames being weak, then I truly fear for all of us. "I've seen him hurt people. You know—you know what he's capable of. Don't mistake his lack of honor for physical weakness."

Celia shrugs that pragmatic shrug that tells me she's already made a decision and won't change her mind. "It doesn't really matter," she says simply. "I know what needs to be done, and I'm more than prepared to do it."

"We have one more advantage," Heath says smoothly before anyone can say anything. Before I can say anything, before I can argue against this insane plan. My stomach is roiling, and as sound and simple as their logic all sounds, I feel like no one is hearing me. "Bernice promises to keep him distracted so he won't have any time to prepare for a challenge."

Now my stomach is twisting for an entirely different reason. I know full well what my mother intends to do, and I hate it. It's a sacrifice she's made a thousand times before, and I suppose this time she has the knowledge that it'll be the last, but it still aches.

Heath nods at me, knowing what I'm thinking, but the rest of the table is quiet. "How is she in a position to keep him distracted?" Bryce asks. "I thought you and your mother scrubbed dishes and did laundry. What exactly is her plan?"

Heath shifts uncomfortably. "I imagine what anyone sleeping with someone does to distract them."

The room is so silent you could hear a pin drop, and it lasts for a long, painful moment before Celia turns to me. "Your mother is sleeping with him?"

Her voice sounds like poison, and it seems to affect everyone at the table. It only takes one moment for my tentative acceptance at this table to disappear. "He's convinced my mother is his mate," I admit quietly.

The silence continues. "Is she?" Callum asks, and I'm slightly mollified to hear more curiosity than vitriol in his tone.

"She says my father is her mate. She's always insisted that. But after Ames killed all the humans in that village and took us, and after she realized we were stuck there... she did what she had to. Ames hates me for what I am and that my father was another man, but I was safe." My voice is quiet, but I force it to be firm. I can be scared, and I can hate having to share this, but I won't have anyone belittle how my mother protected us.

164

"I've never heard of a wolf being mated to someone who isn't their mate in turn," Callum muses.

I shrug. "It's not like Ames is loyal to my mother. He collects lovers like trophies. He doesn't treat her like a mate; Heath can tell you he doesn't give her any real information, not on purpose. He just wants her to warm his bed. Who knows if he really thinks she's his mate or not."

"Your mother has been sleeping with the enemy who wants every member of this family dead for decades, and you didn't tell me," Celia says. Her voice is once again ice cold in the way I hoped was truly done between us.

"It's not a happy story. She's miserable. And she deserves a place here like you promised. I didn't want to bias you all against her." I look to Heath for help because he knew, and he still trusted the information my mother gave him. He knew when he came home, and he didn't consider that the most important piece of information. He makes eye contact with me and gives me the slightest nod, but he doesn't say anything.

"I didn't promise you anything," Celia says.

"Of course you did, I—"

"I didn't," she interrupts me, half-turning away from me. "I told you I wouldn't hurt her if she didn't attack one of mine. She is sleeping with the enemy. If she is with him, if she defends him—then what happens will happen."

My throat tightens and my breathing stutters. It's like I'm looking at a completely different person than the one I woke up with this morning. "You promised," I manage to whisper.

She doesn't acknowledge that and pushes to her feet. "If we wait, we risk losing the element of surprise," she says clearly to her brothers, but she looks at me as she says it. She's implying my mother won't keep Heath's secrets, that she'd turn him in to Ames. I want to argue, but she keeps talking. "Heath, pick who you trust to go in with you. Bryce, you're with me. Callum—" He sits up straighter, eyes on her, taking in her every word. "You can come. Bring your soldiers," she practically sneers the word, "but you're staying at the back. And any argument, I'll tie you up and leave you until we get back to you, get me?"

He opens his mouth, but the look in her eyes silences him. He just nods.

As one, all three brothers stand, knowing their roles now. "And me?" I hesitate to even ask.

"You'll stay here."

The words are simultaneously expected and a slap to the face. "I'm not any more vulnerable than Callum. I can stay at the back, too."

"No." The word cracks like a lightning strike. "You'll stay here. I don't trust you there right now, Bethany."

She doesn't give me a chance to argue, just walking away like everything is settled.

Fuck that. I am her mate. And I know that I don't have great examples of how mates should work, given how Ames treats my mother, but I do know that something changed these past two days. I do know I'm supposed to be her partner, her supporter.

I do know that she doesn't get to treat me like this.

I follow her, dogging her heels and refusing to leave even when someone hands her a saddled horse. "Celia, don't—"

"I'm going to end this," she cuts me off again, her eyes cold. "We can talk when I'm back."

Will I even want to talk to her when she's back? There are some acts that are unforgivable, even between mates.

She mounts the horse and turns sharply away from me, leaving me in the dust as people hurriedly fall into place to follow her. And I'm left standing there, fear making my heart race and grief making my stomach ache, and she doesn't look back.

CHAPTER THIRTY

CELIA

I know I was too harsh on her. I know it within the hour, but it's too late now. I can't turn back.

I have our sorry excuse of an army trailing behind me, joining us as word reaches people, and turning back with all of them would certainly give away any element of surprise we might possess. We all know full well that Ames likely has spies in the forest.

Besides, turning around just for her feelings isn't a viable option. I have to put the security of all wolves and the continuation of the crown over personal matters. One person can't get in the way of that.

I can't cater to Bethany's emotions, and I can't prioritize our mating bond. I can't even spare her mother if she double-crosses us in any way.

Bryce has ridden up beside me, and he's opened and closed his mouth for what feels like a thousand times already. But he apparently won't say anything even if he wants to scold me. And I know why, too. The conversation around our table lingers in my mind.

Today, I have to be braced for a fight to the death, and every other distraction pales in comparison.

I don't think I'll lose. I didn't lie to Bethany when I told her I'm prepared for a fight like this. I always have been. All four of us can fight and fight well, but I'd always had the additional pressure of days like today. I'd always known that, someday, I'd have to fight not just for my life, but for the crown as well.

I doubt Ames is anything too impressive. If he was impressive, then he would have been at my coronation, ready to issue a challenge the minute the crown touched my head. But I know better than to get complacent. A false sense of security will kill you faster than a blade. My father taught me that, and I won't forget it today.

I push faster. I have to believe that Ames doesn't yet know we're coming, and if that's the case, we need to make good time and keep the element of surprise.

This needs to be finished, and the sooner, the better.

***

Heath rides ahead of us, going to send his signal to Bethany's mother. Bernice. I can't think of her as Bethany's mother, not right now, because that just makes me think of the look in her eyes when I was leaving.

It's easier to think of her as Heath's source of information. She's not family or an enemy; she's just a source.

Soon, I'll have to decide what to do with her. But that can't be right now. I'm too emotional, thinking about my mate instead of the best interest of the entire kingdom.

I force myself to put it to the back of my mind. I can't make a decision until I know exactly what is happening in Stone Village.

Stone Village is too uncomfortably close to my own home, and I spend half a moment thinking of what to do with that. Can I trust that these people won't be a threat after Ames is gone? Do I burn the village to the ground and make the wolves here integrate into other villages?

Later. That's getting ahead of myself here. I have to survive the night first.

Heath left his signal for me, a crude crown scored into a gnarled old oak. He's in the village already, then, and we need to be ready.

Bryce and I exchange a knowing look and ready our troops just out of sight of the front gate, leaving a few soldiers at the very back to tend to the horses, hopefully far enough away from the village that they won't be noticed.

Our troops are not the most impressive sight. Callum wasn't wrong to think we needed a standing force again, and he and I will need to discuss that later. But that doesn't mean they're ready for a true war. Hopefully, sheer numbers and shock value will be all we need today.

Callum and I can have a discussion about the future when it comes. For today, I know without anyone saying it that this fight relies on me, not Callum, not Bryce, and not Heath.

Like he hears what I'm thinking, Bryce takes a step closer to my side, and then places the crown on my head. My breath catches; this crown, ancient and time-worn, worn by our father and all of our ancestors, represents the hope of all the wolves. Bryce doesn't say a single word and moves with no fanfare, but I know every single one of the soldiers sees it and knows what it means.

I didn't even know that he brought the crown here. I wore it for my coronation and planned to never wear it again; it's heavy, too big, and not quite comfortable. But it feels right to have it here.

I am going to face a challenge tonight, but it helps to remember that only one of us is a legitimate ruler. Ames is just a usurper, and he'll die like a usurper.

I hold my breath, and I feel like every person around me is doing the same. Come on, Heath. Come on.

Anything could have gone wrong. I've made the decision to send my brother into that village twice now, risking his life both times. He could have been caught. Bernice could have turned him into Ames. Anything could have happened while I was just sitting here waiting.

Then the front gate creaks open, and I breathe again. Heath did it. I see him looking through the gap in the door, a mischievous grin on his face, and everything falls into place. Half the fight is over now. I can do this.

We move silently into the village, wanting to keep the element of surprise for as long as possible. Callum's soldiers do all right at following along, and while I'm only half paying attention to them, it's good to know that Callum has taught them something helpful.

Heath guides us through the streets, confident that he knows where he's going. He spent weeks here, after all. I don't know how he can do things like that and have no one ever be the wiser, but he's always been able to. It's unnerving, but it's helpful.

Unfortunately, he can only take a group as large as ours so far before someone notices our presence. When there starts to be movement in the houses around us, when eyes start to peek outside before ducking back in, Heath points to the hall up ahead, and I know that the time has come.

"Ames!" I shout, feeling foolish but refusing to let it show. "Come out and fight me. If you think you have what it takes to lead, then prove it here, in front of everyone." I wait a moment, then add, "Wolves won't have a coward as a leader."

Howls of agreement sound behind me, Callum's little army somehow sounding five times their size and a thousand times more ferocious. A quick glance shows me some of the Stone Village wolves looking out at us, but I refuse to focus on them. Instead, I turn my full attention to the hall where Ames is. Only Ames is my problem, and he requires my full attention until he's dead.

The only sound for a long moment is my army. Then, at last, Ames pokes his head out of his hall, looking like a coward.

He's physically imposing, even for a wolf, with hair cropped close to his scalp and eyes that dart around quickly, taking in the situation.

I stand tall and firm. I'm here as the rightful queen; he's the usurper. I don't have to justify anything, I remind myself. I just have to stand here and hold steady. "Come and face me," I say, not bothering to shout anymore. We both know he can hear me.

And we both know that every wolf around us can hear me. My people, his people, it doesn't matter; if he refuses, every wolf will know to mark him as a coward.

He steps outside his door, eyeing the army behind me. "You have no right to interfere in matters of this village!" he calls back.

I point to the crown Bryce put on my head. "I have every right. This village is mine."

He takes a step closer; I hold my ground. "I take care of my people."

"Some of your people," I agree, Bethany's face involuntarily flashing into my mind. I shake my head. I can't think about her right now. I can't afford any distractions.

But I can't quite shake her, either. The softness of her smile, those rare times I get to see it. The way those pale eyes watch me. That she lived here, and she hates this man, and has just as much right as I do to hate him.

I stand impossibly straighter. Bethany is mad that I left, but she would want me to do this. She would want me to end him.

"You're a power-hungry despot who will kill anyone to get your way. You'll kill your own wolves to get what you want. You killed my parents, sneaking into our village and luring them out unarmed. You're a snake, Ames, and no one should follow you. You won't protect them when the time comes."

He steps closer. "And they can trust you to protect them?"

I know what he's trying to say; I'm young. Untested. I hold my chin higher. "Yes."

"No one believes you," he jeers softly, but I know every wolf hears his taunt. "You haven't proven anything yet, Princess."

I don't let the reduction of my title rankle me. I don't let his taunts about my age or experience bother me. I know what I am. "Then challenge me properly, coward. If you think you can take on the mantle, prove it."

A challenge is meant to be formal and dignified. There should be rules, a dedicated space, and witnesses. I know that tonight won't work like that.

Ames takes my words as the agreement, this space as the challenge ring, and all the wolves around us as our witnesses. Bryce lets out an involuntary shout when Ames lunges for me, but I ignore him. I ignore everyone but Ames.

Let this be how nature intended it, then; bloody and violent and visceral. We don't need weapons when we have teeth and claws.

I charge him as he gets closer, not letting him control this fight entirely. He dodges, but I expected that, and I weave around him, turning us both around. Now he has my army at his back, and I can't imagine that's a comfortable position for him.

He lunges again, and I dodge, a half turn out of the way. The crown clatters off my head and lands in the dirt between us, and I ignore it entirely.

We circle each other for a moment, never taking our eyes off each other, and then he lunges once more. This time, his claws land in my side and come away red.

First blood goes to Ames, but that's okay. I knew he would strike, and I knew it would land. And in the same way, I knew he'd unbalance himself with the reach.

Each of my siblings could have predicted the exact same thing. I remember practicing what I'm about to do with them and our father a thousand times.

I sweep at his legs, then sink my claws into his back to shove him to the ground when he stumbles. The move puts me off balance, but rather than fight it, I follow him to the ground, landing with one knee on his back and the other in the dirt.

I can feel his skin tear under my claws, and I dig into him deeper, trying to secure my hold on him. He bucks like a wild horse, and I grit my teeth to try to hang on, but his bulk helps him flip us both until I'm on my back and he's over me.

I'm sure the wolves around us are reacting, but I close out the world, only paying attention to right here, right now. I could die in a moment if I don't end this. I've never really feared death before.

The fear gives everything clarity, making the world brighter than I've ever seen it before. I push and buck until I have the leverage again, and I scramble on top.

And there's promptly a bright, stabbing pain in my chest.

I snarl and look down, and Ames is looking intently at the blade sticking out of my chest. He grins up at me, savage and self-satisfied, but I snarl in his face.

He wants to play dirty? That's fine. He killed my parents, who were unarmed and unprovoked; I never expected this to be a fair fight.

When he tightens his grip on the blade and starts trying to drag it into my heart, I lurch backward, tearing his grip off the blade. The pain makes me weak, and the blood makes my fingers slip off the bone handle time and time again, but I grasp it and tear it out, biting back the roar of pain from doing so.

Blood loss won't kill me. I don't think the blade found my heart, but if it did, even that won't kill me. Probably.

"Coward," I manage to say through gritted teeth, then turn the blade in my grip so I can wield it against him. His eyes widen, and he scrambles backward.

The blade is lethally sharp but small, meant more for food than war, but Ames made his own bed. If it hurts when I kill him with it, then that's his own fault.

He scrambles in his boot for another blade, but I'm faster. My knife cuts into his throat, letting the blood spurt like a geyser. He gasps, but it's not enough. It won't kill him, and I need surety.

Only one of us was ever going to walk away from this. And it has to be me.

I slice again and again, deeper each time. This knife will never get through the bone, but that's okay. I don't need to kill him with the knife, just incapacitate him.

He finally grasps the knife in his boot and manages to stab me again. His aim isn't clear, and he misses my heart this time. His grip isn't strong enough to maintain control of the weapon, and I jerk it right out of his grasp, leaving it in my chest as I continue sawing at his throat.

I grab his head, turning him so I'm behind him. "Yield," I demand. He doesn't say anything, although I don't know if he can still talk. I debate asking Bryce for my sword, but I can't have anyone saying that I cheated in this fight. He might cheat, but I need the wolves to look to me after this and still respect me completely.

It would be a kinder death for Ames to have my blade end things cleanly and quickly. And I am not here to give him a kind death.

For my parents. For my siblings whose worlds changed that night. For every wolf he manipulated, the humans he killed, and the people he abused. For Bethany.

So, still aching in pain from the stab wounds Ames gave me, I pull his head back and prepare to rip his throat out.

A force barrels into me from the side, knocking my grip on Ames loose. I shout, trying to roll out from under whoever this is, but I can't turn fast enough.

"Coward!" Heath bellows, and the weight on me lessens. I blink up at Heath, grappling with the wolf who joined the fight. Before I can get my feet under me, another wolf joins the fight, trying to go after Heath.

Fuck, this has spun out of control. No longer even vaguely resembling an honorable fight, this is an all-out brawl.

Bryce is there for the one trying to stab Heath in the back, and I get my feet under me just for a blade to be placed at my throat. Before I can formulate a plan, another blade is there. This time, it's Callum putting himself between me and danger, and he doesn't back down. "Go," he says to me, not turning away from his opponent. "We'll handle them. You have a job to do."

I love my brothers with my whole soul, but I've never loved them more than this moment. These three boys are mine, and they've always had my back. A part of me wants to tell Callum to get back, that he's still too young, but I know better. For better or worse, this is his fight, too. It's our crown he's defending.

And he looks so self-assured right now, so confident that he can handle himself. I nod and don't interfere, moving back toward Ames.

I'm bleeding sluggishly still, but I don't let that slow me. I need to finish this, and soon.

I hear swords clashing behind me, but I force myself to ignore it. They can hold their own while I finish this.

I sink to my knees next to Ames, who is still lying in the dirt, his injuries just starting to heal. I'll never give them time to finish.

I don't let myself think about what I'm about to do, letting the animal inside me take over for a minute. And when wolves need to finish a fight, they go for the throat.

And so I do. I move quick and savagely, far quicker than Ames deserves, and rip his throat out with my teeth, forcing myself not to think of the taste of the too-warm blood and sinew under my teeth.

I spit it out as I stand, sparing a glance at the now-mangled corpse. Blood is still dripping from my mouth as I look back at my brothers, all neatly wrapping up fights with finality.

None of Ames' men are getting out of here alive tonight. The Crae family will walk away from this victorious.

I scan the crowd around me, looking at the wolves who served as witnesses.

Callum is the first one to say anything. "All hail the queen!"

"All hail the queen!" Heath takes up the chant, and the rest of the wolves follow when Bryce scoops up my crown, dusts it off the best he can, and puts it on my head.

CHAPTER THIRTY-ONE

CELIA

I give everyone a moment, but then I turn to my brothers. "Deal with this," I mutter, gesturing to the too-busy street. "I have something to attend to."

Bryce blocks my path. "What's the plan for this place?"

My first instinct is to say burn it to the ground, but I hold my tongue. "We'll know more when we sort through how many of them are still loyal to Ames and his vision of the future. If they can show loyalty to us, then they'll be spared."

"Spared?" Callum asks, huffing. "What, are we executing everyone else?"

None of us react. Callum looks between the three of us. "Seriously?"

"What else can we do?" Bryce asks. He sounds exhausted, and I realize I don't know the last time he slept. I need to get everyone some rest soon. "We can't just let another uprising happen."

Callum looks at all of us but bites his lip instead of arguing.

I knew he was too young to handle this. He might be able to lead his own little army. He might have held his own today. But he's still little more than a child, and thinking everything would be fine now that Ames is dead is childish.

There will probably be more blood before this is over. There's no way to avoid it, really. Not if I want to send a clear message that this little coup is over and that it should never happen again.

I'm tired, exhausted from the blood and death, from this little back-and-forth that only ends in death. I can't show anyone, and I force my spine straighter. Crown on my head and blood on my hands, I need to pretend that I don't doubt any of my decisions. It's the only way to move forward.

"Figure out who can be spared," I tell them, then move around Bryce to do what I originally set out to do. There's someone I need to find.

The door to the hall is still open, so I walk in without waiting for anyone's permission. The place is a mess, and my mind once again goes to Bethany and how ruthlessly she's kept our home clean. Was she responsible for Ames'?

That would be yet another connection to the megalomaniacal asshole that she never disclosed to me, and I'm not quite sure I can handle anymore secrets from her.

There are three young women lying around the place, sleeping on makeshift beds. I peer at their faces, but none of them even remotely resemble Bethany, so I ignore them and leave them to sleep. If they didn't hear the literal battle and the shouting outside, then they need the rest.

Unless... I creep over to one and bend over to check for breathing. Just when I crouch down, a voice behind me says, "They're alive."

I jolt and turn, not having even heard the stranger enter the room.

She's sitting at the top of the loft, looking down the ladder at me and these girls. Her light hair is piled high on her head, as if she twisted it quickly to get it out of her way as soon as possible. Her eyes are pale and sharp like her daughter's, too.

I look between her and the girls. "Then what's wrong with them?"

"Drugged."

"Drugged?" I repeat, the word foreign to me. What could they possibly have ingested to make them drugged? Our bodies burn through most intoxicating substances in a few minutes. We can't even get properly drunk.

She shrugs. "They're young. Once Heath told me he was opening the gate for you tonight, I wanted them out of the way. Ames was less likely to think of using them as human shields that way."

"Would he have?" I ask, swallowing my revulsion.

"Ames? Absolutely." She begins to climb down the ladder. "That's why I sent my daughter away. Ames was always a coward, and he would kill anyone to save himself."

"True." If I know nothing else about that man, I do know that. "So, who are they?"

"They're young. They're Ames' preference of the week." She lands on the main floor, smoothing her skirt before stepping away from the ladder. "There's no window up there. Can I assume you killed him?"

She's so shockingly nonchalant about it that it takes me a moment to answer. "I did. So, you drugged the random girls he dragged in here? I thought he was telling people you're his mate."

Her step stutters, and she freezes entirely for a moment before resuming her walk toward me. "Ames didn't believe in fidelity, obviously." She looks over at the three sleeping girls. "Someone should ensure they get home, if they want it."

"Did he take them?" Has Ames been kidnapping girls, all without me ever knowing?

She shrugs. "It's more like coercion, from what they tell me. He convinced them he could offer them things they wouldn't get at home. Better food, finer goods, silver for their families… you get the idea. Some of them weren't wanted at home. Ames looked like a tolerable option compared to that."

"I can have someone look into getting them home," I say after a moment, not able to stop thinking about what she's saying. My stomach twists, and I force my spine even straighter to hide it.

"Of course, I wasn't involved in those conversations, so for all I know, they really could have needed to get away. This could be the best they've ever had."

I doubt that this village could ever be the best someone's ever had. "I suppose we can ask them when they wake up," I say, trying to keep my thoughts out of my voice. I look at her to gauge if she will share when that might be, but she ignores me.

"Oh, so you've decided what you're going to do with this village?"

"I thought you said you didn't have a window upstairs." That's the only way she could have conceivably heard what I said to my brothers, and even that would have required keen ears.

"I don't. I have common sense, though. I'm aware of what might happen next." She moves away from me and to the table, where there's still a mess from earlier. "I suppose now that Ames is dead, I can clean this… if it's worth it. Will I still have a home in the morning, Queen?"

"Undecided," I say shortly, not liking this line of questioning. "What do you mean, now that Ames is dead, you can clean?"

She shrugs, picking up cutlery. "I'd stopped doing that a while back. When he no longer had my daughter to hold over my head, I said he wasn't getting the privileges of a mate from me when he didn't act like my mate in turn."

"Is he your mate?" I ask, cutting through the nonsense. I can't get her to look me in the eye, but I stare her down, demanding to know the full story.

She goes very still, which makes me think I know the answer. "And how have you been treating my daughter, Queen? Heath says she's part of your family now. I'm assuming you didn't bring her along."

"You thought I'd bring my mate to a battle?"

"I suppose it depends on why you left her behind."

I open my mouth to defend myself, but I don't have to say anything. I owe this woman nothing.

Nothing, except the life of my mate. And that's a very big debt indeed.

I clear my throat and change the topic instead of answering. "Why didn't you flee when Bethany fled? You could have gotten away."

"He would have followed me. And I couldn't do that to Bethany."

That alone is enough to answer the uncomfortable question. "So your plan was to stay forever?"

She shrugs. "He killed your parents, and I sent Bethany to you with all the information you needed to kill him. I imagined it was a matter of time before something happened to him. And here we are."

She sounds so blasé about it all, and it makes my muscles tense and my blood boil. "So you thought we'd come to rescue you?"

"Or I'd continue to hold my own. Whatever happened, I was happy to get Bethany out." She actually looks at me now, holding her ground.

"You used my parents' murder to benefit you."

"I didn't see any other opportunities coming to save us," she says. Her voice is even, but her tone is dripping venom. "No one was coming to check on our well-being here."

"We leave the villages to themselves."

"Admirable. Except when despots like Ames take power."

That I can't argue with. "Bethany wants you to come home with me."

She tilts her head. "And what do you want?"

That is a good question, and I don't insult it by answering too fast. "I don't trust you," I admit.

She sits at the table, and I do the same. "All right," she says slowly. "I didn't expect you to, I suppose."

"He killed Bethany's father... and you slept with him?"

"You sound like you disapprove." I don't dignify that with a response, just watching her until she gives in and sighs. "What do you want from me, Queen? Forgive me for wanting to survive."

"He murdered your lover, and you let him call you his mate." I wait a moment, then press. "Is he your mate?"

"Is the answer going to change how you feel about me?"

"It could. To be his mate..." I shouldn't let my feelings show, I know, but I can't entirely help it.

"We don't choose the people in our life," she says. "But we can choose how we react. And I had a daughter to protect."

"What happened?"

Her shoulders fold inward and her head dips toward her chest. "You're not entitled to this story because you're mated to my daughter, you know."

"No," I agree. She's making herself smaller, and I do the opposite; I make myself bigger, leaning over the table enough so she can't escape my presence. "I'm entitled to this story because I'm the one who decides whether you get to come home with me or if I leave you in this village to burn."

She looks up at me abruptly, taken aback by the threat. Her mouth opens to retort, but then she freezes like that, her eyes trapped somewhere over my shoulder. I tap the table once to get her attention back, but she doesn't move.

I turn, realizing there's a window behind me. The chair makes a screeching noise as I shove it back to stand, but I ignore it and move to the window. Who is eavesdropping on us that she's so interested in? I stick my whole head out, looking left, then right, but I see no one.

"Who are you staring at?" I demand.

She's silent for another moment, but then clears her throat. "No one. I... no one." There's prolonged silence for a moment, but then she says, "All right. I'll tell you."

I'm not even remotely satisfied with this concession, and I remain standing by the window in case I can catch whoever it was.

"But you should know it won't help you," she says. "My daughter might seem sweet and soft, Queen, but we both know she's stubborn as anything under that, don't we? And you can threaten me all you want, but if you want your story to end happier than mine, then you have a ways to go."

"Just tell it," I say shortly, not in the mood to be lectured by a woman mated to a murdering monster.

"Very well," she says. She gestures to the table. "Come sit."

Chapter Thirty-Two

Bethany

I don't even consider staying behind.

I'm smart about leaving; I'm still rational enough for that. I don't join Callum's soldiers or walk right up to Celia and demand that she take me. I don't follow right behind them, giving myself away.

I wait a few hours. I let Celia think she left me behind, that I'm no longer a problem that she has to worry about because, apparently, that's what I am to her. I thought we'd repaired whatever was broken between us, but it's clear that this gap is too big to close right now. Or maybe ever.

She's threatening to kill my mother for who she sleeps with. And what's worse, I made it very clear that it's all under duress, and Celia does not care.

I know she's never fought for her place somewhere. That she's always belonged and known it, that people have never dared to not respect her. That she fundamentally doesn't understand where I come from.

I just thought that being her mate meant that we could get through that. I thought fate would never give me someone who would be such an obstinate, stubborn ass about only seeing the world through her own limited point of view.

I don't care what I have to do. I don't care if I have to smuggle my mother out of that village, stand between her and Celia, or face down an army, but I'm not going to let Celia have her way on this.

The problem is that they left on horseback, and I didn't even think to steal a horse, if there even is a single one left in the village able to make the journey.

At least I know where I'm going. Or, more accurately, I can follow the rather obvious path left by all the soldiers following after Celia. Any idiot could follow this path, which is excellent because I have to admit I couldn't find my way back to Stone Village under my own power.

What must it be like to have a skill like Celia's and always know your way home? Not that I truly consider Stone Village home, but I was raised there. I lived there for over three decades.

I have my too-large sword and some food I thought to bring along, but not much else. I don't have a plan for when I arrive. I don't have a plan for what to do or where to go if I really do need to rescue my mother from my mate.

I should have brought more food. I should have remembered that I'd barely eaten for two days and now am once again marching through the woods on a nearly empty stomach. My stomach rumbles, but I don't dare to stop and find food. I have no idea what's happening in Stone Village, and I need to make up as much time as I can.

I don't know I'm getting close until I see that damned stone wall. I stop short, ducking behind a tree to survey the situation. There's no sign of Celia's army, although I suppose there wouldn't be. She would never just stand her army outside the gate; she'd have some sort of plan.

When I don't see them hiding in the trees either, I move slowly through the trees until the gate is in sight, and for the first time in my memory, it's thrown open.

I don't enter through the gate; that seems like a good way to walk into something I'm not prepared for. Luckily, I know another way in.

The river is rougher than I remember, but I make it across and through the crumbling wall. Once I'm in the city, I can hear the noise of the streets. It's the middle of the night; there should never be this many voices unless something has happened.

It's over, then. One way or the other, it's over.

I pray to the gods that everyone I love is still alive. My mother, Celia and all her siblings, Honor and the other soldiers. Let Ames rot. I know the gods don't answer prayers, not anymore, but I can hope that this one they'll see fit to grant me.

I'm more than used to moving around this village unobtrusively. Good help is meant to be neither seen nor heard, and I've gotten more than used to living like that. I sneak around the perimeter, dodging everyone who might be out tonight, and make my way to Ames' hall. Whatever happened, that's where I'll find my mother.

There's a window in the back that's a little bigger than average, and there's a rock beneath it that I placed there years ago. It's at the perfect height for me to boost myself inside, and I've used it for years whenever Ames didn't want to let me in or out. I approach the window nearly silently, listening to see if I can get any clue what happened tonight.

"You're not entitled to this story because you're mated to my daughter, you know." That's my mother's voice, and if she's talking about my mate, then Celia must be with her.

My heart starts pounding. I didn't realize Celia would go right to my mother. She must have won the fight with Ames, which means one danger is past. But I assumed she'd celebrate after, or perhaps discuss the governing of this place with Bryce and Heath. I never thought she'd immediately go after my mother.

I need to get in there, to interrupt and make peace between them. But just when I put my foot on the stone, Celia says, "No. I'm entitled to this story because I'm the one who decides whether you get to come home with me, or if I leave you in this village to burn."

I freeze entirely, halfway to the window. She'd threaten my mother? She'd really go that far when it's so obvious my mother is more Ames' prisoner than his mate? If the attack worked, it meant she helped them. That alone should be enough to win Celia over.

But it's not. Just like she promised back home, she will grant my mother no mercy, no forgiveness for the perceived fault of who she sleeps with.

My mother's eyes widen. She's clearly seen me in the window, frozen in place, trying to decide what to do.

Her eyes flick to the side, and I know she means for me to run again. But I won't be sent away without her this time. I won't let Celia make this decision without having to face me.

Her eyes flick to the side again, insistent now, and I realize she's very purposefully looking east. And while I have no memory of ever being there, I know what's to the east.

I was born that way. She used to point it out when we watched the sunrise, quietly telling me to remember where I came from whenever Ames wasn't listening. My mother wants me to go back there. My mother wants me to go home.

Praying she'll meet me there, praying she has a plan, and this is not just one more attempt at self-sacrifice, I turn and disappear around the side of the building.

CHAPTER THIRTY-THREE

BETHANY

I didn't expect to find an actual village here. But I suppose, for humans, the destruction of this village was practically a lifetime ago. After a while, you rebuild and move on.

I wonder if the humans buried the bodies somewhere else or if they decayed where they fell. Maybe my father is in this soil somewhere, and I can't decide if that's comforting or terrifying.

I chop wood and cook and catch fish, and I find a quiet, accepting community that invites me in. Everyone in this community seems to keep their head down, and their philosophy seems to be that if you work, you eat.

It takes two weeks for my mother to find me. My heart never quite beats normally until she's here. I think she told me to go here, but we never previously agreed on a signal for this type of thing or even for running away from the village in general. And even if she did mean for me to go here, I can't ignore the threat Celia made before I left.

I'd like to think that I know Celia better than to believe the threat. She's my mate, after all. But how well do we really know each other? We've barely spent any time together, and I felt like we were making progress at the full moon, but everything that's happened since makes it clear that we haven't.

But my mother shows up, removing a scarf she must have used to hide her hair, as light and recognizable as mine. "Sorry," she says, stepping up to my side where I'm trying to catch enough fish for dinner. "They were keeping an eye out for me."

"Are you okay?" I demand, immediately abandoning my fishing net to stand and turn to her, trying to check her for injuries. "Did they do anything to you?"

She brushes my hands aside gently. "Darling, I'm a wolf. Short of killing me, there's not much they can do." She looks at me sidelong. "And they don't want to kill me. Your mate knows better than to risk it, even if I don't think she likes me much."

"It didn't sound like she knew better," I grumble, thinking back to what I heard that day.

"So you only heard that small portion," she surmises. "You didn't stick around to hear more."

"You told me to run."

She sighs. "That I did. It seemed the best option at the time, although now I wonder... I was wondering if you'd come here."

"You told me to." I didn't imagine that look, did I? I didn't imagine the times we watched the sunrise, and she whispered about where I was born. "Did you not want me to?"

"To tell the truth, I think I just wanted to. It's not the best place for either of us." She frowns. "Ames never let me come back. Not even to bury the dead. And now... well, it's not the same."

"It's a nice place," I offer, trying to cheer her up even though I know nothing can change everything she lost. "I think you could be happy here."

"It's not the same place," she murmurs. "Your father and I, we lived in a hut right over here," she says, gesturing to where a few young saplings are growing now. "And our neighbors, right over there... she made beautiful clothes. And she told the funniest stories." Her eyes are distant as she moves around, and I know she's trapped in her past.

I can't give her the past back. I can't give her back the years she's lost in the meantime, either. But I can offer her now.

"Do you want to stay here?" I ask her.

She shrugs. "It's not really an option, is it? Humans are fragile. They grow old, they die. You and I..."

"I'm pretty fragile," I mutter with an unexpected amount of bitterness. She gives me a sidelong look. "Sorry, it's been an issue. Between Celia and I."

"And that's the other reason we can't stay. You have a mate," she concludes.

"Like you had a mate?" I dare to ask. I've avoided it for three decades, but now I need to know.

She goes very still. "You heard more of the conversation between your mate and I, then?"

"No." I had run when Celia turned toward the window, with absolutely no desire to be caught in Stone Village. I left town as quickly as I could, knowing if I stayed I risked being caught, and then I'd never get away. "What conversation?"

"How'd you know he was my mate, then?"

Because I'd had a lot of time to think since I'd run, and thinking about the past is easier than worrying about the present. Because I have a mate too now, and all the pieces fell into place. "You wouldn't leave him because it hurts," I say instead of answering. It all makes sense now, every time she didn't leave when I thought she should have. Every time I thought we could leave, but she found an excuse to stay. I know how it feels now, and I'm not sure I'd have the strength to choose this again.

"I'd done it once, and it had hurt terribly," she admitted quietly. "It was worth it, but I always knew I wouldn't be strong enough to do it again."

"I'm surprised you're doing as well as you are right now." Mate bonds can sometimes kill the other partner. And if they don't, the pain is unmanageable for a long time.

She sighs, and moves to sit right on the ground, gesturing for me to sit with her. I do, crossing my legs and watching her, feeling like I'm a little child and she's going to tell a story again. "Sometimes fate gets it wrong, it seems. Or we do. Ames was…"

"A monster," I finish for her.

"A man who started truly thinking he had good ideas," she corrects me. "And was willing to give anything for those ideas. Including others' lives, their freedoms… he would do anything. He loved power more than he loved his good ideas. And when I saw what he was becoming—I left."

"And you met my father."

She nods. "And you were conceived not long after. To tell the truth, when you were born, I was worried about whose baby you were. I didn't even know if I could have a baby with a human. But it became clear very quickly. Fully wolf babies might be mortal when they're born, but you were more delicate than any I'd ever seen. You had human blood, and you had your father's nose."

I squeeze my own thigh. I never knew that. Never knew there had been any doubt about my parentage, that Ames might have for even a moment thought he had any claim to me. I suppose he got over that, with how he treated me as I got older.

But I suppose that just proves my mother's point. If he had been a decent mate at all to her, he would have raised me as his own. He would have shown my mother he could give us a stable home. And he chose not to, and now we are where we are.

"I liked him," my mother continues, heedless of my thoughts. "He helped me when the separation was too much, although he never knew what was truly making me feel that way or even how bad it was. I never told him. I debated it, but before I came to a decision, well, you know what happened."

There's ash under our feet, only barely covered by new growth. We both know what happened. "Ames wanted you back."

"Yes."

I swallow, thinking about all the humans who died because Ames wanted my mother for himself. Like property, I think sourly. Like he had the right to come in and take her. "All those humans…" I begin, but then decide not to say it. It's too much. "You told me he killed this village because he wanted their supplies for the winter."

Her fingers dig into the ground around her, and she nods. "I never lied to you. You believed it because you've seen it, darling. Ames did kill humans because he thought they were beneath him. Ames looted everything he could get from this village because that was the practical thing to do while expanding his empire. He did it all the time, and no one would have thought this time was any different. But he took you and me as well. He thought I was his mate. But I didn't feel much like his anymore. We have a choice in it, Bethany darling. Fate decides who would suit us best, but if we change… then fate was misled."

"I know," I whisper, feeling like I do. Sure, my mother's mate murdered her lover and treated me like a servant and murdered his king and queen and tried to manipulate others so he could rule them. She clearly is in the worse situation out of the two of us. But my mate threatened to murder my mother, and while she clearly changed her mind, I can't forget how much she never wanted me. How I was an inconvenience to her.

She said I'd never understand the pressure the crown put on her, and I've given up trying. She can manage that all on her own.

"The story had an impact on your mate, too," my mother says slyly, a little smile breaking through her melancholy.

"I don't want to talk about her right now." I do wonder where she is—if she burned Stone Village to the ground like she threatened, or if she went home. If she's making everyone into her enemy once more, or if Ames' death has helped her settle down. But no, that's not my place anymore. She's made it clear she doesn't want me there, and I don't want to continuously punish myself by trying. I can take the hint, and I can do better for myself.

"That's up to you," my mother says. "I'll tell you whenever you're ready."

"What if I don't want to think about her at all anymore?"

She gives me a long look, one that I think sees right through me. "Oh, darling. I remember the pain. And it's quieter now, with so long since I loved him—but it never goes away. You'll want to be with her if it's at all possible."

"That's not a good reason to be with someone," I point out.

She's quiet for a minute, then nods. "No, it's not. And if you're so noble that you'll leave her to make a point—more power to you. Let's see if she can change your mind." And with that final pronouncement, she pushes herself to her feet and dusts herself off, extending a hand to me. "Show me what else has changed," she offers me, and I let her pull me to my feet, taking this distraction for what it is.

CHAPTER THIRTY-FOUR

CELIA

I can't shake the feeling of dread pumping through my veins. I don't deserve to shake it, either.

What I did to my mate, what I'm becoming—I can see it so clearly now. I can see the path I've set down, and I can see where it ends, clear as the blood on my hands. I don't deserve to feel better until I beg my mate's forgiveness.

"Where is she?" I ask Agnes, storming into her little yard, disturbing chickens as I go.

I'm tired and hot, and smell like horse and blood. I haven't bathed or even changed clothes since Stone Village. I haven't had the time or the inclination; I had to solve the issue of an entire village of possible dissidents, all while all I wanted was to go home as fast as I could. I rode home hard, determined to see my mate and to start to clear the air between us. I've been aching for her like a missing limb, my heart yearning to begin to bring things back to how they were before Heath brought the news to us, and now I can't find her.

I need her. The burning, pulling feeling in my chest has only gotten worse, and I need to make things right. I've been an idiot. No, worse than that. I've nearly ruined what I've been given. I have to be able to fix it.

Agnes looks up, eyebrows raised, her nose wrinkling at my smell. "Not here. I haven't seen her in days."

"What do you mean, not here?" I'm aware I sound rude, but I can't help it; my heart is in my throat, and I need Bethany now. "She was supposed to be here. Where else could she go?"

Agnes shrugs and actually turns away from me. "I don't have answers for you. I'd assume she was not so forgiving of being left behind."

I run out of her yard without another word. She clearly doesn't have anything of substance to tell me, so I march back to the hall, hoping there's an obvious sign I missed there.

Callum and Bryce wait for me there. Heath is still in Stone Village, acting as my representative until I decide the best course of action. I'm not going to burn the village to the ground, but that is the only option I've ruled out so far, and I need someone I trust to keep an eye on the village in the meantime.

"Any luck?" Callum asks.

"No," I snarl, stalking around the place as if I'm going to find her just around the corner.

"She can't have gone too far," Bryce comforts. The words do little to settle me; this isn't the first time she's run away, and she could be absolutely anywhere by now.

"Want me to go back to Stone Village?" Callum asks. "See if she's shown up there now that she knows it's safe?"

My worry is she didn't wait for it to be safe. That she foolishly put herself in danger just because she was upset with me.

"Fuck," I snap, and both of my brothers immediately turn to me, my outburst taking their full attention. "I thought Bernice saw someone who surprised her. I didn't see them, but..."

"She knows the village better than you," Bryce acknowledges. "She could hide. When was this?"

"The damned night I killed Ames."

"Do you think she's still there?"

"Doubtful," Callum says. "We went over every inch of that place."

Yes, we had. I'd wanted an exact inventory of everything Ames had possessed, and I'd needed to know if he'd hidden any more girls other than the ones he coerced into his home.

Those three are Callum's age, and all three elected to stay in Stone Village, which makes them Heath's problem for the time being. They don't seem to feel particularly strongly one way or the other about Ames' death, but I warned Heath about them. Not that he needed the warning; he knows full well that every single wolf in that village is a potential threat.

Which is why we'd combed the entire village. I'd needed to know every item, every hidey-hole, and every person. I'd needed to know exactly what kind of place Ames was running. We'd gone through homes, interviewed villagers, and demanded total transparency before we left.

Bethany might know the village, but no one knows anywhere well enough to evade an entire army that puts the fear of death into every citizen wandering around. No one would have protected her, especially since, from what I've heard, no one protected her when Ames was alive, either.

"She's not there," I say with finality. "She went there, but she left."

"To where?" Callum asks doubtfully. "She doesn't have anywhere else to go."

"That didn't stop her when she ran away last time she was mad at me, either," I point out. "She'd just started walking."

"You found her then."

"She didn't have a multi-day head start."

"She's your mate," Callum says, voice rising with the tension. "She's your damned mate, it shouldn't matter how long it's been. You should be able to feel her anywhere."

Bryce rolls his eyes. "Now is not the time for bedtime stories, Callum."

Far from looking ashamed at Bryce calling out his childish impulses, Callum just looks more determined. "Tell me I'm wrong," he challenges me. "You can find this place across the world; you're telling me you can't find your mate?"

I turn away from him, but not because I'm ignoring him. I just need him not to be staring at me like that while I try.

The truth is, I could recognize that tart, sweet berry scent anywhere in the world. Bethany smells like home just as much as this village does, and I'm fully aware that I've done a poor job showing her that so far.

I broke her trust. We were building something, something beautiful and new and very, very tentative, and I broke it the first chance I got. I got scared again, and I did what I always do; I closed her out.

I'll fix it. I'll find her, and I'll fix what's broken between us, because I'm fully aware that I won't succeed without her.

You can push a mate too far. Bernice taught me that, and I cannot have Bethany and I repeat history. I won't be Ames in this scenario.

I take a deep draw of air. It's not that I can clearly smell the sweet berry scent, but perhaps there's the slightest hint of it on a breeze.

If I'm imagining it, then I'll ride around until I actually smell it, even if it takes days. Even if it takes weeks or months. I'm not giving up on us so easily.

"Bryce, you're in charge until I return," I say, already leaving out the door. I'm not waiting for another moment.

CHAPTER THIRTY-FIVE

CELIA

I find my way back to Stone Village, where Heath is waiting for me with a raised eyebrow. "I didn't think you'd lose faith in me this fast."

I ignore the jab. Maybe I deserve it, maybe I don't, but either way, I can sort out how my siblings feel about me and my reign after I find my mate. "I'm looking for Bernice."

"I was surprised you left her here," he admits. "I thought your mate would want her with us, since, if I remember right, that was her original goal anyway."

"Bethany is missing," I interrupt him. I deserve the scolding about how I treated my mate, but I don't have time for it. "Gone. Did she come here?"

Heath's good-natured poking instantly fades away, and he immediately stands up straighter, eyes more alert. "Missing?"

"She left. I don't know where," I admit. I hesitate for a minute, then say, "I was... not being the best mate. I'm sure Bryce and Callum told you I haven't been the best sibling, either."

"Not my place to say," he says shortly, not making eye contact with me, which makes me believe he feels it absolutely is his place to say and probably will say something as soon as we have a moment together where I'm not half-panicked about losing my mate.

"I need to find her, Heath." Let him think me pathetic; at this point, I am pathetic, and I don't care.

"And you want to ask her mother."

"Bethany loves her. She wants nothing more than to have a home with her mother."

"And are you going to offer her that?" Heath asks shrewdly. "Since you left her here and all, I could see why Bethany would worry."

"Bethany doesn't know I left her here. Unless you saw her?"

"I wouldn't keep it from you if I did." He turns away, leading me back toward the home where I met with Bernice, where she shared with me her whole sorry history. Where she impressed upon me how badly I need to not end up like her.

There's still a hollow feeling in my gut when I think of her story. I don't even know any wolves who have rejected their mate. I know wolves who have survived alone after their mate died, but Bernice is the first I've met who rejected their mate. And I will not be the second.

Heath knocks respectfully. "Ladies? Bernice?"

One of the young women who Bernice drugged before the fight opens the door. She's so painfully young, and I hate to think of what Ames did to her. Of the promises he made a young woman to lure her here, and how he treated her.

"Is Bernice here?" Heath asks.

"No," the girl says slowly. "Hasn't been all day."

"All day?" I snap before I can help it, and she flinches back. I try to rein myself in, and Heath steps in front of me like he thinks I need to be separated from the child. "She left?"

"Where would she go?" Heath asks, sounding much calmer and kinder than I do.

The girl shrugs. "She didn't say anything. She just left."

Heath turns to look at me. "She's not here anymore, is she?"

"No," I agree. "Now I have two members of our family to find."

***

It takes days to track her scent, following it through the forest and across a river, until at last I end up outside a human village.

I slow my horse and think that over. I know what Bernice would say about that. I know she'd say relentlessly tracking Bethany's scent is exactly how Ames came after her.

Bethany would probably say that I'm not any better. And while I, at the very least, can say that I have no plans to kill anyone to get my way, I know I'm uncomfortably close to Ames and his views.

The bastard is dead, and at my hand. No one can deny that I killed him with honor. That should mean his views and his ways are dead now too, but I'm all too aware that's not true.

The people who chose to follow him because of what he promised them don't want those things less now. When this is over, Bryce and I need to plan how to win over the villages all over again, and I know I have work to do to make it actually effective this time around. But the worst problem is me. When Bernice talks about Ames, I hear my own thoughts, my own actions. And I simply can't let that be true.

Bethany was the only one who called me out. I know my siblings tried, but they've been told since birth that their job is to support me as queen someday. Their criticisms were always going to be quiet and too easy for me to ignore. But Bethany isn't bound by the same constraints. Bethany, breakable, gentle-hearted Bethany, looks me in the eye and tells me that I'm failing at this and that I need to turn to the people around me to do better.

I need her. And I hope she needs me.

No, that's not quite right. I hope she needs me, yes, but I don't want her coming back just because she needs me, because I ease the ache of separation or help her sleep, or that I provide a home and access to safety. I hope she wants to return and that I give her more than just some simple, physical need. I hope she looks at me and sees someone she wants, a future she craves.

That's where Ames' mistake was, I know. He thought his sheer presence should be enough for Bernice. He thought power and a village of his own would make her want him. He thought he could make her so reliant on him that she'd have no choice but to cling to him, and it makes me sick. Because he's a disgusting waste of space, yes, but also because I know how close I was to doing the same thing with Bethany.

It wasn't on purpose. I never set out thinking that I could make her reliant on me. I never planned to take everything from her until I was all she had left. But I know I did that, or at least started to. And I need to make up for it.

I dismount the horse before entering the village. This is a human village, and I don't need to be any more physically imposing than I already am. Humans can usually tell that we're different, and even if they don't know precisely why, there's usually some fear in them. It's best not to add to it.

"I'm looking for two women who showed up in the last few weeks," I tell a nearby man. "Hair as light as snow, eyes like cold river water…"

He nods, his time-roughened skin crinkling around the eyes. "Aye, I've seen her. She's a helpful one."

My heart aches because, yes, she was helpful in our village too. She's helpful because she doesn't know how not to be, because she hasn't known a place that wants her just simply for existing.

I should have given her that. We should be partners, both working for the betterment of our home and our village. But more importantly, she should never have felt like all that mattered was her work.

"Where would I find her?"

He points, and I nod in thanks, following his direction to a decrepit-looking hut. "Bethany?" I call as I get close, because surprising her feels like the wrong choice.

When someone emerges, it's Bernice, giving me a long, cold look. "If you hurt my girl again, I won't hesitate to step in."

Bernice is taller than her daughter, more imposing, and more wolf-like. Nevertheless, I know I could best her in any combat scenario. Despite that, the icy look in her eyes lets me know that I won't win this time. Honestly, I don't think I'd even fight. If I hurt Bethany again, I'll deserve what's coming to me.

I take a deep breath. "I'm here to make things right," I promise her.

She studies me for a moment, then nods. "Go, talk to her. Fix things. She's hurting, Queen."

I shudder at just the thought. I knew she must be because she hurts when I hurt, and I haven't slept properly since the full moon. But knowing it abstractly and hearing it are different. My mate should never be hurting.

I nod and nod again in thanks when she takes my horse from me. Then I walk inside, hoping I can fix this between us.

Chapter Thirty-Six

Bethany

C elia looks a mess.

Her eyes are frantic, her short hair sticking up in every direction, her clothes travel-worn and still bloody. I frown just looking at her, immediately standing and abandoning the stew I've been cooking. "What's wrong with you?" I ask before I can stop myself.

"What's wrong with me?" she asks, taking another step closer as if compelled. "Do you want the entire list, Bethany? I'm too controlling, I don't listen well to others, and when I panic, I retreat into myself and don't take advice well. I haven't been the mate you need or the queen the wolves deserve, which is a shame because I thought I could handle at least one, but I've failed all the way around. I—"

"Stop," I interrupt, holding up a hand. "I didn't mean—you don't look well," I say lamely.

She nods. "Yes, and for exactly the reasons I just listed. Being a poor mate to you has made doing anything else difficult. And I see now how I hurt you.

I'm here to fix things." She takes another step forward. "Bethany, I shouldn't have left you there. I shouldn't have said what I said."

Her eyes are so earnest that I take a compulsive step forward. "Celia, I—" I trail off, not knowing exactly what I want to say. I can't forgive her. I'm not ready yet. I look away from those pleading golden eyes. "I don't blame you for putting your crown first." It comes out slightly begrudging, but I don't mean it to. I don't begrudge her her duty to the crown. I know full well that being queen means something to her. I met her on the day of her coronation, after all—it's always seemed like the crown and our mating bond are side-by-side in her life. I just have never understood why exactly she shut me out.

She takes another step toward me, stopping just at the limits of my reach. She gives me space, but I know it's hurting her. "Fate gave me you because we're perfect for each other," she says quietly. "We'll complete each other in a way no one else ever could. We'll make eternity not only bearable but worthwhile. But you and I—there's more than that, Bethany. I've always been told that I have to live for something bigger than myself, and I've tried, and I know I haven't been successful. But I should have understood from the beginning—if you're my mate, then you're not just perfect for me. You're perfect for the kingdom. You're meant to be here with me, at my side. I need you, Bethany, but so do all the wolves."

I fall to sit in the only chair in this place. "That's a lot to expect of someone, Celia."

"I know," she acknowledges, and her chin dips down in guilt. "Would it help if I promised some things in turn?"

"I don't know. What are you promising?" I feel like I'm out of my own body, that this conversation is happening to someone else. Maybe it's a dream. I pinch myself, then wince. No. Still hurts.

Celia steps closer again, kneeling on the packed dirt floor and looking up at me. "If you are my mate, Bethany, then you are my equal. I treasure your input. I want your support, and I'll support your dreams in turn. We are a unit, tied together, and we'll work like it."

I turn my face away because if I have to look at her, I'm going to immediately give in. "Even if your mate is a fragile little half-human?"

"My mate is the strongest person I know. She bruises and she gets cold, but she never stops. She does what she has to. And she left me when she knew it was the best option for her, showing that she's far stronger than I've ever been."

I have to keep looking away. I have to—my eyes are filling with tears, and my throat is closing. Does she know how long I wished to hear anything like that?

"I won't stay if I don't think you're keeping your promises," I say when I feel like I can control my voice.

"I invite you to beat me over the head before you leave."

"I won't stay if you don't start listening to people. Not just me. Your brothers. The people you interact with—everyone has ideas, Celia."

"What you and Agnes were talking about, let's start there," she says seriously, like we're in some form of a council meeting, instead of her still looking up at me from her knees. "But you can decide if that's before or after we visit the villages again. I need to do better."

"We?"

"I'm not traveling without you again. It hurts. And if we're going to do this together, then we'll do it together."

"What are... why now?" I ask hoarsely. "This is everything I wanted to hear, Celia. Why now?"

"Because your mother told me the story, and I refuse to be Ames all over again. I see his failures, and I'm scared of how easily they could be mine. I always thought you got that way with evil in your soul, but now I understand it's not like that. All it takes is selfishness and inaction. And I won't let myself follow that path." She hesitantly sets her hand on my knee, the most gentle touch, like she's unsure if I'll accept it. When I don't move her hand, she relaxes slightly. "I'm not saying that I won't make mistakes, because I will. But they'll be my mistakes, not his. Will you be at my side when I make them?"

"You have to keep your promises," I tell her one more time. "You have to—don't shut me out again, Celia."

"I won't. Ever. That's a promise."

"Then—yes," I say, once again choking up. I've never been this close to crying so often in my life, and I go to wipe the tears away when Celia leans up on her knees to stroke her thumb over my face, wiping the tears away herself.

"I got you," she says softly. "You're okay. We're okay."

I can't hold back the tears, and Celia continues to stroke my face as I cry. When I at last get a hold of myself, I take a big sniff and ask, "What happens now?"

"Now, we go home. Unless you need something here?" she asks.

I shake my head. No, any history I thought I'd find is gone, buried under ash and new growth. I don't remember this place any more than a stranger would.

"I want to go home," I admit, and it feels like something falls into place inside me when I say it. Home. Our home.

"Then we'll go home. We'll meet with my siblings and probably half the village too, and start talking about changes. All the things I promised you I'd do, we'll do them. I know you were talking about trade, Callum is worried about the military, and Bryce likely has thoughts about how exactly I should plan to approach the other villages. And of course your mother should come with us, and—"

"Yes, that part isn't going to happen," my mother announces, strolling back into the hut.

I start. "Have you been listening the whole time?"

She shrugs, completely unrepentant. "If she'd upset you, I wasn't going to stand by and let that happen. I'm glad you patched things up, darling, but I won't be going home with you."

"Where will you go?" Celia asks while I'm reeling.

"Back to Stone Village. Ames was an unrepentant murdering despot, but the people there aren't. And many of them came because he promised them things. The girls—do you know that Elsa is half-human too, just like my daughter? And the other two don't have anywhere else to go, Queen. They fell for Ames' lies for a reason. We are not the only wolves who have felt unwanted." She stands up to her full height, eyes firm with her determination.

My heart swells again. I've never seen my mother like this. I've known she's determined, and strong, of course. I've known for a long time what she's done to keep me safe. But the fire in her eyes now is new.

That fire in her eyes shows a woman who knows she has a future and can see it for the first time in a long time.

I turn back to Celia, watching her swallow as she pushes to her feet. "Then Stone Village is yours. Consider yourself the new pack leader. And as for the unwanted wolves—when we reach your village, be prepared to talk about how I can help them. No wolf is unwanted."

My mother looks at Celia for a long moment, then nods. "Take care of my daughter," she says quietly. "You can start there."

"Yes, ma'am."

I watch them looking at each other for a moment, then stand so I can tug on Celia's hand. "We should go, right?"

She gives me a long look, looking down at my hand softly before making determined eye contact with me. "If you'd rather go with your mother to Stone Village—"

"No," I interrupt. It hurts to know she'll be somewhere else, but she's doing what she feels she needs to, and it doesn't change anything. I still know where my home is. "We're going home. You made me promises, Celia."

She squeezes my hand. "Then we'll go home," she agrees. "It's time to start this. And do it right, this time."

CHAPTER THIRTY-SEVEN

CELIA

True to her word, Bernice stays at Stone Village. She walks back into the home that was once Ames like she owns it. I suppose she does, considering everything. Certainly no one else is more entitled to it.

As far as I know, the three young women are still living there. "Do you want to meet them?" I ask Bethany. "They seem to be your sisters now."

"I'm sure I will. Eventually. When we come back this way. Stop trying to give me chances to get away from you, Celia. I don't want them."

I squeeze her lightly where she sits on the horse in front of me, grateful beyond measure that she's so fully committed to coming back with me. Heath is going to join us too, so we five Craes can sit together and determine a plan of action.

And I'll listen this time. I'll hear what they have to say.

I know my brothers. I'm starting to get to know my mate, and I like to think I'll know her better soon. We have work to do, but I'm confident that the five of us can get it done.

Heath comes out with his own horse, eyeing us skeptically. "You're really riding all the way home like that?"

If he knew what it felt like to be physically separated from a new mate, he wouldn't question this one bit. As it is, the idea of having Bethany more than an arm's reach away makes me ill.

Heath just chuckles. "Don't blame me when you're slow."

"Heath?"

"Yeah?"

I grin. "Ride ahead. Tell the others we'll be there when we can."

***

"Why are we stopping?" Bethany asks me when I'm confident that Heath is far enough ahead and Stone Village is far enough behind us.

I kiss the side of her neck before hopping down from the horse, helping her down after me. "I know I promised we'd get to work on fixing this mess when we get home. But we're not home yet, are we? A few minutes before we have to take things seriously—that sounds like something else we need, yeah?"

She smiles, winding her arms around my neck and pressing a teasing kiss to the corner of my mouth. "It's a good plan."

I smile, then turn my head to take a real kiss from her, making her moan before I pull back. "I know it is."

"So, what did you have in mind?"

I look up at the sky as if contemplating my plan right now. "I figure, Heath already thinks we're slow..."

"Yes..."

"So, if we're still home by morning, he won't ask too many questions."

She tilts her head back too, looking up at the sky. "Oh, so we have a few hours, hm?"

I grin wickedly, hiding it in her neck as I already start sucking a bruise there. "Plenty of time to make you scream."

***

True to my word, she screams until the tree branches shake. I lick her until her voice starts to fade, and when I finally have to stop, I press kisses to her soft thighs, then up over her hips.

Her hand finds my hair again, scratching at my scalp in a way that makes me go boneless. I rest my head on her stomach, and if I didn't know any better, I'd say I was the one who just had three orgasms in a row from my soft, peaceful contentment.

Well, that's not precisely true. My cunt tingles with need, and I'm still aching for her. But her hands on me are enough for right now.

I summon the ability to lift my head and look her over. She looks soft and relaxed. An irrational part of me, more beast than woman, feels a purr of satisfaction seeing her like this. I did this. I provided for my mate; I made her feel good, and I made her want to be here with me.

My eye catches on the bruise I sucked into her neck. "Next full moon, I'm putting my mark right there," I say. "Will you mark me back?"

Her fingers continue to stroke through my hair. "You know I will."

I kiss her stomach. "Then I'll be the happiest wolf in the world. Now. I don't want to make my brothers wait too long. They might stop believing we're just slow, otherwise." They'll smell Bethany on me the minute we walk anywhere near them, but I don't bring that little fact up.

"What about you?" she asks.

"We can save it for later." It truly hurts me to say that, but that the best course of action is to wait. I hold firm and put the needs of the pack first.

I do have the ability to be the kind of self-sacrificing queen the wolves need, after all.

***

The look Bryce gives me when we finally ride into the village would terrify a lesser wolf, but I just hold my head high. One day, he'll understand why I'm late, and I look forward to reminding him of today when that day comes.

"Family meeting," I say shortly, helping Bethany off the horse. "Five minutes. If everyone isn't there, get them there."

He just stares for another moment, then snorts and shakes his head. "We've been waiting on you."

"Good. Five minutes." When he doesn't move, I stare him down. "You can go now."

"Demanding," he grumbles, but he walks away.

"Celia," Bethany admonishes, "be nice to your brother." She tries to say it with authority, but I'm already backing her against a fence, so her words lose some of their power.

"Bryce knows what I mean," I dismiss, running my nose down her neck. "We've been talking to each other for seventy years. It's fine. We'll be fine."

"Even so." She sighs, tilting her head back and letting me kiss her skin until she seems to shake herself out of it. "Enough. We can't be any more late."

"I'm the queen. I can be whatever I want."

"I think that's what caused the problem in the first place."

I sigh. She's more than right, and I still just want to kiss her.

Being a new queen and having a new mate is incredibly difficult, just for different reasons than I originally assumed.

"Fine," I say, stealing one kiss before finding her hand and leading her inside.

Chapter Thirty-Eight

Bethany

I don't quite know what my role is at this table, but Celia has made it more than clear that she wants me to be here.

No, not that she wants me to be here. That she expects it. Needs it. That it's critically important that I be here, representing some faction of wolves I can't even imagine.

Each of us takes a seat around the table, with Celia at the head. My first instinct is to get up and make some food—I'm hungry, but it's also a job I'm very used to having—but Celia gestures for me to sit in the seat next to her, so I force myself to sit there and listen.

I take a deep breath. This is my place now. I am a part of not only the family, but of this little court, too. This is what being Celia's mate means, and I'm going to be ready for it.

Celia takes a deep breath. "I know I haven't run this pack like you all hoped for," she begins. Callum opens his mouth, and Heath punches him in the leg. Celia pretends she hasn't seen. "I know. It's been a... difficult adjustment."

"For all of us, Celia," Heath says reassuringly. "No shame in that."

She tilts her head. "This isn't the type of thing that I can say no shame about. If I make mistakes big enough, people get hurt. So, I want to try again. I want to fix this."

"Tell us the plan. We're listening," Bryce reassures her.

"I'm not going to do this alone," she says. "Callum, your idea of a standing army has merit. I'd like to think there are no more threats to us, but I think we all know better. The rest of the wolves could use the security of knowing we are ready to handle any situation that might arise in the future."

Callum nods and uncharacteristically keeps his mouth shut.

"But you're very young. This will be your task, but I don't want you near the front line of a war." This time he can't resist, but Celia just keeps talking, and doesn't give him a moment to interrupt. "I won't lose one of us, and you are one stab wound away from bleeding out. In a decade or two, it'll be yours. For now, Heath can work with you."

Heath raises an eyebrow. "I'm not much for leading, Celia. That's always been you."

"For now, you are. You can do anything for two decades," she says firmly, and I see the leader in her. Firm and in command, and expecting her vision to be executed, but there's still a kindness in her. She hears him, and I know she'll work with him. But we both know she's still in charge. "Callum will be at your side, so I imagine you'll have time for other tasks."

That gets his attention. "Good," he says, leaning forward slightly. "Because we might think the army is a good idea, but that doesn't mean everyone will. And I think we need to start feeling out what people are thinking."

Celia nods. "That's exactly what I was hoping for. Just to gather information—this isn't a hunt for dissidents. Just to understand people. Perhaps you can identify some problems for us to fix."

Heath grins. "That's exactly what I do best."

"And me?" Bryce asks, leaning in now.

"I think we need to revisit the tour of the villages," Celia says. "You, me, and Bethany. And this time, the three of us should talk first. Bethany has a lot of ideas about what we should be doing to support the villages, and I imagine you do, too."

Bryce looks at me for a long moment before nodding. "I'm excited to get started."

Celia nods, looking around the table for a long moment. "Good," she says, tapping both hands against the table. "We start tomorrow then. Everyone, find somewhere else to be for today."

The three brothers look at each other. "Find... what?"

"You heard me. Everyone out." Celia rolls her eyes. "It's the middle of the morning. Go, be busy."

"You're seriously kicking us out? None of us had breakfast, you know. We were waiting for you."

"Boo-hoo. Find it somewhere else."

"Celia," I begin, blushing furiously.

She holds up a hand. "Give me a minute, sweetheart."

Heath breaks first, snickering and standing. "Well, we've been told. Let's go." He looks the two of us over with a smirk. "We can get started on work while you two... rest." The emphasis he puts on rest sets off a new round of blushing.

Callum and Bryce follow him out, and Celia waits for the door to click before standing and pulling me up as well. "You didn't have to kick them out," I scold, her hands already tugging at my waist.

She stops moving for a second. I'm expecting her to lean in for a kiss, but she doesn't, just watching me instead. "We've never done this before, in this house. And this is where my mate and I belong."

Something in me melts entirely at that, and I lean in to demand a kiss from her, which she eagerly returns. "Take me to bed, then," I murmur, and she doesn't need further direction.

She gets my clothes off, and I tug at hers, until we're both naked and she tumbles me into the bed. I groan, letting my head fall back into the softness surrounding me. Fuck, I missed this bed.

It's like Celia can read my mind. She kisses my collarbone, murmuring, "Ours forever now," and then starts kissing down my body.

But I vividly remember last night—and this morning—and I'm not going to let her control this between us again. I might not really know what I'm doing, but I've learned what kind of touches make Celia melt. I roll the two of us until I'm on top, straddling her thighs and cupping her tits, teasing at her nipples until she arches up into my hands.

"Bethany..." Celia says, warning evident in her tone, and only slightly ruined by the breathiness of her gasp.

I grin at her, liking this. Liking her falling apart for me for once.

I move my hands from her breasts, across her shoulders, then down her arms before gathering her wrists and gently moving them over her head. "I'm going to make you feel good," I tell her.

She just stares up at me, not trying to break my admittedly weak hold. "Okay."

"And you're going to let me."

"Okay." Her throat bobs when she says it, but her eyes are half-lidded, her body soft and pliant beneath mine.

My hands are busy holding her arms in place, so I improvise, working my thigh between hers and pressing softly against her cunt. Her eyes flutter shut and her mouth falls open. She needs this, needs me, and the knowledge of that makes my own cunt clench.

I move my thigh just slightly, pressing a tiny bit harder, and I manage to work a moan out of Celia. I do it again, then begin to rock my thigh against her, rhythmically giving her what she craves.

She tries to rock against my thigh, and after a moment of fumbling, she finds what she's looking for, gasping something that sounds like my name as she does.

"You're so wet for me," I murmur, feeling the hot, sticky mess she's leaving on my thigh. "Are you close, Celia?"

She grinds against me particularly forcefully, then sighs. "I've been wet all day," she murmurs. "You think I can have you come on my tongue and not walk away wet?"

"You should have let me take care of you then."

"Some things are better if you wait. I wanted it to be—fuck—here. I wanted this bed. Our place. I wanted to show you—this is real now. No more stolen moments in the woods."

"Well," I say, daring to release one of her hands so I can play with her nipple again, "maybe some stolen moments in the woods. They're not all bad."

She gasps when I pinch her nipple, already rapidly nodding her head. "True, true, I—yes, you're right. A mixture of both." I release her nipple, and she sighs. "But I wanted to start here."

And that's sweet in a way I can't quite describe, in a way I didn't know Celia could be. I release both of her hands so I can put mine on the bed, leaning down to kiss her.

She eagerly returns the kiss, using her newly freed hands to her advantage, taking my face in her hands and holding me right where she wants me. She grinds down against me, but breaks the kiss with a moan. "More, I need—more, Bethany. Please."

"All right, all right," I soothe. I'll give her anything she asks for right now. The only problem is I don't exactly know how. "What do you want?"

She smiles, slow and lazy, her whole demeanor shifting. She rolls her hips languidly against my thigh and says, "I want your fingers inside me. Now."

I trail my hand down her body, sitting back on my heels to watch her body break out in goosebumps as I move my fingers teasingly along her skin. I reach her hips, and she actually growls at me. I laugh but do move to her spread thighs.

She spreads them wider for me, tilting one knee up to give me the perfect view of her. "Give me two of them, sweetheart."

I slide two fingers inside of her and can't stop my eyes from rolling back with the warm, tight heat of her. She groans, spreading her thighs even wider as if she needs to give me a better target.

"That's it," she gasps. "Turn them, crook them upward, like that—oh, fuck." The words come out drawn out and breathy, and triumph rushes through me, warm and demanding. I did that. I made her eyelids flutter, her muscles tense, and her breathing change.

I don't need instructions for what to do next. I watch her face, eyes rapt with her blissful expression, and know exactly how to touch her. How to please her, how to make her melt entirely for me.

"Sweetheart, I'm going to—" I don't get any more warning before her cunt squeezes my fingers, her thighs closing around my hand to hold me exactly where she wants me while she screams my name to the rafters.

When she starts to relax, I carefully withdraw my fingers, licking them clean and letting my eyes slide closed at her sweet taste. Fuck, I want to taste more. I'm already moving, lying down on the bed and lifting her knee over my shoulder.

She pushes lightly at my head. "Not going to give me even a moment to recover from that?"

She made me come until my mind simply melted away last night. I think turnabout is completely fair.

The moan she lets out when I lick through her folds is enough to shake the bed frame.

CHAPTER THIRTY-NINE

CELIA

Bethany, to my eternal annoyance, decides the appropriate thing to do is get up and make breakfast in the morning.

I concede that we probably can't fuck any longer, but I also argue that with some time for recovery and a nap, I could make her come again. Unfortunately, my mate seems to think that the promises I made yesterday need to begin right now and that it's her duty to ensure I get started.

When I'm upright and can smell food cooking, I can possibly admit that she's not wrong. I made promises, and removed from her intoxicating scent and touch, my brain once again starts to turn over plans for the future.

Bethany isn't the only wolf who doesn't meet our typical expectations of a wolf, and she's not the only one who's been hurt by how we treat wolves like her. How many are there? How can I best help them?

Then there's the trade between the packs that more than one pack leader mentioned when I was traveling, and the trade within the pack Bethany and Agnes talked about. And Callum isn't going to take me ousting him from his military position lying down, so I'm going to have to find creative ways to keep him occupied for the next decade or two. And Bryce and I need to make a plan for exactly how I should be speaking to the villages, one that we can both live with, because I cannot afford a repeat of the last time.

Footsteps outside our room draw my attention away from my thoughts, and I finish lacing my clothes before going to join my mate.

Only to find all three of my brothers sitting around the table, looking like they're eagerly waiting for breakfast.

"You ruffians just expect free food now, huh?"

"Are you really the one to call us out for that?" Heath says, smirking. "I noticed you weren't out here cooking."

"I like cooking," Bethany interjects, bringing dishes to the table. "We can work out who does what around here later."

That I like the idea of. That makes us feel even more like a family.

I tug Bethany into the chair beside me as soon as her arms are divested of plates. "Anyone needs anything else and they can get it themselves," I say to her, but meaning for the entire table to hear it.

"Speaking of decisions about how this household works..." Callum says, and I already know I'm not going to like what comes next. He seems to know it, too, not having the courage to finish his thought.

Bethany remains oblivious. "Yes?"

"We all came to a decision last night," Heath picks up the conversation.

"Oh? I don't remember coming to a decision."

Callum snickers. "No, but you remember coming to some other things, don't you?"

Bethany being right here is the only thing that stops this from turning into the type of knock-down, all-out brawl the three of us older siblings got into plenty when we were small. "Figure out what you want to say," I order him through gritted teeth.

Bryce rolls his eyes. "We want you two to move upstairs."

I blink. "Our parents' room?"

"Yeah."

"Why?" The idea feels slightly wrong, truth be told. That space has always felt sacred to us, somewhere removed from the rest of the home. Barring an emergency, we never went up there. It was their space, and we respected that.

"Because you're loud as fuck, and we want to sleep," Heath says.

I blink, taking that statement in. "You listened to us?"

Callum spreads his hands as if defending himself. "You all fucked for nearly an entire day. Did you expect us to not come home last night?"

"A perfectly valid option," I say through gritted teeth. I turn to Bethany, trying to see how she's taking this conversation over the nice breakfast she made for us, and of course, she's blushing furiously, ducking her head.

"Be reasonable, Celia," Bryce says.

"I am being reasonable."

"And so are we. No one else is sleeping up there. You'll have your space. We can sleep. Everyone wins."

Bethany reaches for me and squeezes my thigh, and I turn my attention fully away from my brothers. "Are you okay with this plan?" I ask her, keeping my voice as soft as I can. My brothers are no longer a part of this conversation; this is just for the two of us.

She hesitates a second, still blushing, but then she nods. "Like Bryce said. Everyone wins, right?"

I doubt it'll solve the noise problem as much as my brothers expect it to, not with how loud I intend to make my mate scream on a regular basis. But it feels like a fair enough compromise. Never let it be said that I don't try to give them what they need.

"All right then," I proclaim, turning back to the table as a whole. "We have a lot of work to do today. But first, we're starting with moving our things."

"First, we're starting with breakfast," Bethany corrects me.

I look around the table at my family, at my brothers and my mate, at the people who forgave me and still stand beside me. My heart, already rendered vulnerable when Bethany let me take her to bed last night, goes completely soft.

I take her hand off my thigh and squeeze it, then kiss her knuckles. "You heard her," I tell the table. "First, we start with breakfast."

Epilogue: Bethany

Present Day

I watch Celia as the others all leave us, keeping a careful eye on her as she gets up to pace.

She does her best not to let the others see her like this, but I'm different. She hasn't tried to shut me out in centuries now.

"This could be big," she murmurs after a long minute.

"Mhm."

"Maybe one of the bigger threats that we've ever dealt with."

"Yes," I agree, getting up and walking over to her so I can take her hands in both of mine, stopping her movement. "And isn't it interesting that it comes when there are eight of us now?"

Four siblings and four mates. Four full houses, each and every one of us fully dedicated to the wolves and this pack.

"What are you trying to say?" she asks, agitated now, wanting to get back to pacing.

This might be the biggest threat, but it's not the first. I know how to deal with Celia's anxiety now, and use my grip on her hands to draw her into me, letting her go only to take her into a hug. "I'm saying we're ready for this, Celia. You're not doing this alone."

"That I know," she murmurs, giving into the hug and holding me close. "Never alone when I have you."

"That's right," I agree, squeezing her. "Is it time to plan?"

Her arms tighten around me. "Not yet. Hold me for another minute first."

I press a kiss to her forehead. "Of course. For as long as you need."

ALSO BY ADDISON JAMES

Crae Romance

Callum

Bryce

Heath

Celia

Silas

Estrid

Supernatural Christmas

A Werewolf for Christmas

A Recipe for Love

Standalones

The Heat Cure

Dragon's Treasure

ABOUT THE AUTHOR

Addison James is a romance book author from New England. They are obsessed with all things mythical, mystical, and magical. A lifelong fantasy reader, that evolved to fantasy romance as they grew up. Addison always has a story to tell and is excited to introduce you to their world of fantasy romance. Addison can be reached through Tiktok, Instagram, or Threads (@Addyjameswriter), through email at addyjames@addyjameswriter.com, or through their website, www.addyjameswriter.com.